The Glow
Book One

Helen Whapshott

www.helenwhapshott.weebly.com

Published by Little Bird Publishing House

London

ISBN-13: 978-0-9567395-8-2

DEDICATION

"Look, Mum and Dad, I did it!"

"LEARNING TO LOVE THE GIFTS YOU'VE
BEEN BLESSED WITH."

ACKNOWLEDGMENTS

Thank you to my folks, you've always believed in me.
Big thanks to all my lovely Twitter and Facebook followers
and friends, who have shown such kindness and support. I
hope I do you proud.
With thanks to Kitty and Katie at Little Bird Publishing House
who have helped me realise my hopes.

1. WHAT IS A GHOST?

What would you do if you saw a ghost? Would you ignore it hoping it would just fade away? Would you go up to it and see if it needed your help? Would you even know you were actually seeing a ghost? Because not all ghosts walk around moaning and groaning, wearing old-fashioned clothes, carrying their head tucked underneath their arm, you know. Mostly ghosts think that is a rather out-of-date thing to do, and those few who still do it, only do because it's become a kind of ironic trademark: a silent self-amusement.

Most people don't know exactly what a ghost is, and if you're one of them don't worry; it's not the sort of thing they teach in schools, nor is it the kind of thing parents usually sit their children down and talk about. People don't like to think too much about it. It kind of creeps them out. Not me. I know a lot about ghosts. Let me fill you in.

When the human body dies, the soul leaves it. How

1

does it do this? Well I'm not entirely sure but there are several theories; maybe it comes out of the nose or mouth, or perhaps it seeps out of the skin though the skin pores like sweat – it's not really important; it's just important that you know that it gets out. When it's out it then travels to the other side, which has lots of different names, (none of them wrong). They exist like the countries of this world. Sometimes however, a soul is reluctant to travel into that strange and wondrous world of the afterlife and instead it stays here, in the world of the living, and these are the poor souls we call ghosts.

And I see them. Everywhere.

Yeah, I bet you're thinking I'm a bit crazy and all that – but it's true, it really is. It's just the way that I was made, so to me it's a little bit crazy that you don't see ghosts. Let me tell you a little more and then maybe you'll understand.

You see, a soul is made up of energy, and it looks exactly like the person when they're alive. Sometimes you can see through them, which can be a little bit creepy, but this is just because their energy is low and they can't show themselves properly. A soul will never fade away completely, they're like a pulsing star, shining strong and bright at times and then pale and wisp-like at others, or if that isn't clear enough, imagine that a ghost is a radio station (now bear with me on this one) Imagine a radio station emitting signals into the world. You can only hear the music clearly if you're tuned in rightly.

There are people who will catch glimpses, blurry figures that are seen just out of the corner of the eye, and then there are those who see ghosts and spirits all the time. These people give off a light, like a candle in a dimly lit room. Ghosts, spirits, and others who belong to the supernatural and paranormal world can see this and they call it The Glow.

2. MEGAN

If people were asked to describe Megan Webb, they would say that she didn't look very special, which was a surprise being that her parents were both very attractive, special looking people. Her dad, Dr. Theodore Webb, a medical doctor, was a tall and incredibly handsome man, with black grey-streaked hair and a face that looked more at home on the cover of a fashion magazine than a hospital ward specialising in general medicine; even if it was at the best hospital in London. Her Mum, Cheryl Webb was also very beautiful. She looked very much how you'd imagine a fairy-tale princess to look, and if this wasn't glamorous enough she had also once owned her own shop where she sold dresses that she had designed herself; that was until her youngest child was born and she gave up work to look after him.

Megan was tall and thin, with chestnut hair that had the habit of sticking up all over the place, no matter how many times she brushed it. Megan always looked pale and drawn. On a good day you could say she was a plain child.

It wasn't until she was thirteen years old that her life as she knew it changed forever. She'd always sort of known that everyone had something special about them; maybe something big that the whole world could see or something so small that only their family and friends could see it. Megan believed the thing that made her special was her art. Whether she was using paint or clay, she was pretty good – maybe even good enough that her work would go into a gallery one day. She had no idea that she was special in ways she hadn't even thought of.

The day Megan's life began to change hadn't been a particularly good one.

It had started that morning when she'd discovered (only after she'd poured it all over her cereal) that the milk had gone off. Her alternative breakfast plan of toast had failed when it burned and set off the fire alarm. It was at this point she conceded defeat against the clock, because she'd already overslept due to pulling a late-nighter doing the homework she'd forgotten was due in the morning (on pain of death). All of this meant that she wasn't in the best of moods when she got into school. She found it almost impossible to concentrate on her English work, couldn't make any sense of Maths, and got smacked in the face in P.E. with a football (All before the lunch bell had even sounded) The day was finished off beautifully by Mathew Den throwing her schoolbag up onto the school roof. Who would have thought that the boy had such an amazing throw? He could make a serious career of being a shot-putter; he was certainly built like one. Megan had to wait almost an hour for the school caretaker, Mr Brown, (a man who clearly didn't like children) to get her bag down for her. He spent the whole time moaning at her as if it had been her that had made the decision to just go ahead and throw her bag onto the roof.

Megan was glad when she got through the front door of her house so that she could kick off her shoes and take a breather. She smiled at the sound of muffled voices coming from the kitchen and the warm, welcoming smell of home-cooking. She walked through the hall and pushed the kitchen door open. Tyler, her baby brother, beamed as soon as he saw her and opened his arms wide. He looked so much smaller than other two-year-olds she had seen; he had the face of a cherub, with big blue eyes far too big for his face, and blonde curly hair. She kissed him gently on the cheek, and then looked at her Mum who was taking some cakes out of the oven. Hearing her daughter, she turned and smiled. Megan noted how every kitchen surface was covered in cakes, biscuits and buns, and she felt her heart sink. Whenever Mum was really worried about something, she would bake – a lot. The last time there had been so much baking, Mum had been building up to tell her that her cat Whiskers had to go and live with Nan and Granddad because his fur wasn't good for Tyler's asthma.

Megan remembered all too clearly what it looked like when Tyler had had his last asthma attack. His lips and fingernails had gone blue, he'd wheezed and coughed, and couldn't catch his breath; his inhaler seemed to take an age to work. Megan had felt like the entire world was ending. She couldn't stop crying and as her Mum screamed down the phone to tell the ambulance to hurry up or her son would die, she felt as if she were about to throw up.

Megan loved Whiskers but she loved her brother more; she never wanted to see Tyler suffer like that again so she made no fuss when Whiskers left. Three weeks after the rehoming he was ran over and killed. Megan couldn't help thinking he'd been trying to make his way home to her.

"Hello darling," Cheryl said, breaking Megan's thoughts. "Had a good day?"

Megan knew it was best to tackle what was bothering her Mum head-on and get it out of the way – like a plaster covering a scraped knee it was better to rip it off quickly than peel it off slowly. She took a deep breath and asked, "What's up Mum?"

Cheryl carefully placed the cakes onto a cooling rack before giving Megan her full attention. "I've got sad news about Great Aunt Betty," she said.

Great Aunt Betty was her paternal grandmother's sister, who wasn't anything like Megan's quietly spoken grandmother. Like clockwork, Great Aunt Betty visited at Christmas and birthdays inevitably bringing garish hand-knitted socks or gloves for presents. She was a stout woman, with a face like a bull dog; her grey hair scraped back into a tight ponytail that made Megan's head hurt just by looking at it. She smelt of cigarettes and coffee and always laughed loudly at her own jokes. The last time Megan had seen her was at Granny's eightieth birthday party. She had poked her fingers (which had long garishly coloured nails) hard into Megan's ribs and exclaimed, "Bloomin' heck! Look at the state of you! All we have to do is put you in the corner, bung a lampshade on your head, and no one would know you were in the room."

She'd then thrown her head back and roared with laughter. The word 'bitch' sprang into Megan's mind and she had to bite down on her tongue to stop it springing out.

She grimaced at the pain in her ribs and the wicked old woman rolled her eyes, muttering something about how Megan didn't have a sense of humour.

That's when Megan's Dad stepped in and said that Megan had a wonderful sense of humour and there wasn't anything wrong with his daughter's physical shape. Great Aunt Betty sulked for the rest of the party.

"She died," Cheryl said as casually as possible, still fiddling with the cakes.

"Oh," Megan said flatly. She didn't know quite what else to say. She knew that normally when a member of your family died you were meant to feel sad, but she didn't; she really hoped that didn't mean she was a bad person. She turned her attention to the relatives that she did have affection for. "Are Dad and Granny okay?"

"Of course Gran's upset," Cheryl replied, "after all, Betty was her sister; she's bound to feel the loss."

Megan often wondered why when someone died people called it "a loss." Surely, when you lost something you didn't know where it was. Most of the time when someone died you knew where they were – unless they'd died in a war, like Sarah's soldier-brother, Peter. Sarah was Megan's best friend, and Peter was MIA. Sarah had factually informed her that MIA meant, "Missing In

Action, which meant dead but that they couldn't find the body." Sarah had punctuated the statement with a string of silent tears. Megan hadn't known what to say, so she had simply held her friend until their shared tears had stopped. Megan listened patiently. Their form tutor Mrs Priest, had reassured Megan that was all she could really do.

"Dad is upset because your Gran is upset," Cheryl continued. Megan wondered if her Dad hadn't particularly liked Great Aunt Betty either. Cheryl picked up a brochure that was covered in icing and cake-mix and held it out to Megan. "Your Dad has inherited her hotel."

"Great Aunt Betty had a hotel?" Megan blinked in surprise.

Cheryl nodded. "Yes, it turns out she was a very rich lady."

She hadn't looked like a very rich lady – rich ladies, Megan was sure, looked like the queen, with nice clothes and pearls, not shabby jumpers, jeans, and basketball hoop earrings.

Megan took the brochure from her Mum and looked at it. The hotel looked horrible, it was a mass of turrets, keeps, imposing walls, and gargoyles. Made from a strange looking black stone, it was covered in ivy. It was the perfect home for a vampire, or a hideout of a mad-monster-making scientist. The brochure informed her that it stood just outside of the Hampshire town, Threshold in the county town of Samhain (pronounced Sowain). Megan glanced over the tourist blurb learning that the 'charming, historic hotel' could be found nestled in a nook of hills surrounded by ancient heath and woodland. 'Threshold', the brochure went on, 'is distinctive in its historic status. The whole town is under a National Trust order, ensuring no new buildings look modern, and could only look like they were from the Tudor, Stuart, Georgian, or Victorian era. The series of glossy photos showed a town full of interesting and old- fashioned shops, museums and galleries (most dedicated to the rich local folklore) that brought in the coach-loads of tourists all year round.

Cheryl reached over Meagan's shoulder and poked the image of the gloomy looking hotel. "Great Aunt Betty lived in that tower there, so that's where will be going to live."

Megan blinked – had she just missed part of a conversation? Did her Mum just announce that they were going to move into what must be the ugliest part of the ugliest building?

"What?"

"Dad and I have talked it over and we think it's the best thing to do," Cheryl replied. "The air will be better for

Tyler and..."

"Better for Tyler!" Megan pointed to the part of the brochure which went on and on about how lovely the heathland looked, and how wonderfully mysterious and magic the ancient woodland was. "It's the countryside Mum, it will be full of pollen and animal fur! It'll make his asthma worse." Megan's head was reeling. She looked at the grim hotel with an impending sense of doom.

Cheryl shook her head and said matter of fact, "Actually pollen has never been a problem."

Megan sighed. "That's because we've never been anywhere where there's a lot of it. And what about me?" Megan protested, "I'm your kid too! What about what's best for me?"

"Megan!" Cheryl looked at her daughter in surprise.

"I gave up my bedroom so Tyler could be nearer to you and Dad," Megan said feeling a hard lump growing in her throat. "I didn't even complain when you gave away my cat." She paused momentarily, feeling a previously unfelt resentment rising. "I didn't even blame you when he was ran over!"

Cheryl flinched at Megan's unexpected anger but Megan wasn't finished. She knew that if she didn't get it all out now then the decision would set like concrete and there would be no chance to change things.

"I've lived in London all my life and now you're telling me that I've got to leave all my friends behind to go and live in a place I've never heard of – to go to school where everyone's probably known each other since they were babies, and to top it all, we've got to go and live in some run-down, Gothic monstrosity that's probably haunted! "

"You'll make new friends," Cheryl said gently.

"I don't want new friends!" Megan snapped. "I like the ones I've got!" She had known most of her friends from their time in nursery. She couldn't believe Mum thought she could leave them just like that. They weren't like shoes that you outgrow; they were like her family.

"I can live with Gran and Granddad and come and see you all during the school holidays," Megan said desperately.

"No!" Cheryl shook her head. "We're a family and we're not going to be separated."

"Doesn't matter if one of us is unhappy," Megan muttered as she picked up her school bag. "I've got homework to do." She hoped that her dramatic exit offered a final comment on the situation.

Once in the sanctuary of her room, Megan threw

herself onto her bed, buried her face in the pillows and cried. It wasn't fair. Ever since Tyler had been born, the whole world had revolved around him.

'Maybe they love him more because he's really theirs and I'm... I'm adopted,' she thought. She twisted her mouth in irritation. She knew that she *wasn't* adopted – well as much as anyone ever knows – it just felt like somehow she was the odd one out of the neat little family triangle. She couldn't put her finger on what it was exactly that made her feel so different, but there was definitely something. She shook her head, no, that wasn't true, she'd always had a very strong imagination she reminded herself, just as right now she was imagining Whiskers sitting on her feet, which was what he always did when she was upset. Megan didn't look up, she knew he wasn't there, but just for a little while, she decided to pretend he was. After a short time, she started to wonder how strong her imagination actually was because she was certain she could hear Whiskers purring.

3. STONE TOWERS

The hotel was aptly called *Stone Towers*. The cold, wet moving day didn't help Megan's mood at all. She spent most of the journey from London staring glumly at the raindrops running down the car window. Despite her parents' overly cheery tourist-guide chat about the beauty of the rugged heath and hills, Megan refused to look for more than a quick glance before sullenly deciding it was nothing more than a full grey sky, lifeless greens, depressing yellows, and boring browns. The scrapbook her friends had made her as a going away present lay on her lap and every now and again she would stroke its cover with her fingers. She tried not to cry.

Megan sat next to Tyler, who was in his car seat playing with his shoelaces. Megan found it very hard to be angry with him. Okay the whole move was because of his asthma, but as Sarah had pointed out, when Tyler got older there would be things he'd probably really want to do but their parents would refuse because of *the asthma*.

"Me-gan," Tyler said waving his sock at her. "Sock." This was Tyler's favourite game; even the thought of his little cackle made Megan smile.

Megan leaned forward and sniffed the sock dramatically. "Peeeeeew," she groaned. "That stinks!"

Tyler threw the other sock at her, which landed on Megan's cheek. She held it in place and whimpered in a squeaky voice, which she knew always made Tyler giggle, "Oh noooo, my face is melting aaaaawaaay, aaaargh!" Tyler clapped his hands. "That's it! Laugh at your big sister's misfortune."

Cheryl turned in the front passenger seat and looked at them, smiling. The sound of her children's play always made her feel content.

"The hotel will be coming round the corner in a minute," Dr. Webb said.

The "minute" felt more like an hour to Megan, and when Stone Towers did eventually come into view, Megan felt her heart sink further. It looked even darker and more uninviting than it did in the photograph.

Dr. Webb, who was known as Theo to his friends, parked the car just outside the front door of the tower they were going to live in. The fairy-tale of Rapunzel sprang to mind: the idea of being trapped forever waiting day after day for rescue. Megan fell out of the car, pleased at least to stretch her legs and studied the door that lead to her new life. It was made of a thick, dark wood and studded with black nails. Megan's eye was drawn to the imposing doorknocker; a metal hand holding an apple core.

"Isn't it impressive!" Theo stated as he rounded the car to give Cheryl a hug.

Dad seemed genuinely pleased to see the building and she wondered what would happen if she broke the spell by telling him exactly what she thought about the place.

"It's very big," Cheryl said quietly. "God knows what it's going to be like to clean!"

"Aunt Betty had someone come in every morning to help," Theo replied. "I'm sure they'll still want their job, and Megan will help, won't you darling?"

Megan prickled, not sure when exactly she was meant to fit in cleaning between school and homework. Clearly she wasn't expected to have a life. She'd learned over the last few weeks that there was no point protesting, so she nodded.

"Good girl." Theo patted her on the head. "Let's have a look inside shall we?"

The front door opened into a commanding entrance

hall. The floor was the same stone grey as the Hampshire sky and the wainscoted walls were finished with depressing dark green wallpaper. There were oil paintings and a wide sweeping staircase, at the bottom of which proudly stood a suit of armour that guarded a loudly ticking grandfather clock. Megan found the sound of it strangely reassuring as otherwise she could have quite believed she'd stepped into a place where time never moved.

She peered into the distant corridor, which was so long that it faded out into shadow. Along the length of it Megan saw doors standing opposite each other like proud wooden soldiers. She opened the nearest door to her on the right. It was a living room, no cheerier, even though the curtains were open. Just like the hallway, the room was full of dilapidated mock-Tudor grandeur. The walls were covered with a forest-scene tapestry. Although faded by the weak sunlight, Megan still found it fascinating. As well as various wild animals, like rabbits and deer, there were also fairy-tale creatures hidden amongst the trees. Megan shook some weird thoughts away and continued her exploration. The furniture looked like it should be in a museum, and Megan wondered why on earth her Dad had insisted on selling their nice modern looking stuff – at least it would have made the place something like their home. Then her eyes fell on the mantelpiece and she found herself staring in surprise. There was a framed photograph of her taken whilst she was drawing, and next to the photograph was a painting of a waterfall Megan had done when she was on holiday in Scotland with her grandparents. She had given it to Theo to put in his study.

"That's the picture I gave you," she said looking up at her Dad.

"Yes, I know, Great Aunt Betty saw it when she came for a visit," Theo replied. "She liked it so much I gave it to her."

"But I gave it to you," Megan reminded him.

"I know," Theo said, "but it would have made Aunt Betty sad if I hadn't given it to her."

By the tone of her dad's voice Megan could tell he didn't understand why Megan was so upset by this and she couldn't be bothered to explain, instead she decided to ask another question.

"Why is there only a photograph of me and no one else?"

"Obviously it's because you were her favourite." Theo sighed. "I don't understand why it would bother you so much."

Megan was genuinely taken aback by the revelation.

She had thought that Great Aunt Betty hadn't even liked her, not alone thought of her as a 'favourite'.

"Megan, could you take Tyler upstairs to explore?" Cheryl asked.

Megan could tell by Mum's voice that she wanted to talk to Dad alone. Megan nodded and took Tyler by the hand. They walked up the stairs slowly and found another long corridor with four doors with a window opposite them. Megan lifted Tyler onto her hip and pushed open the first door, which was an antiquated bathroom. With its puke-green suite, it gave an entirely new meaning to shabby chic.

The next room wasn't much better. With its garish bright yellow walls, bare floorboards, and a small desk and chair in the corner it looked sickly and miserable. It didn't invite further exploration. The next door was different from the others, long and narrow. Megan guessed it was a cupboard, so she skipped it, and moved onto the next; the room was even bigger than the yellow room, with a stately wardrobe, a rather grand four-poster bed, and a dressing table.

Theo's voice came from behind her and made Megan jump. "So, what do you think?"

Megan turned and looked at him. "Aunt Betty didn't die in here did she, dad?" she asked.

He smiled though Megan didn't think it was very funny. "No, she died in a teashop in town."

Megan thought that must have been horrible for the people who worked at the shop, and those who had been sitting at the tables nearby.

"Which rooms are me and Tyler going to have?" she asked.

She hoped hers was going to be the yellow one, because although not exactly perfect, it was next to the bathroom and she hated the idea of having to roam the creepy corridor at night.

"Tyler's having the one next to bathroom, and I think I've found the perfect room for you," Theo said grinning.

"Is it downstairs?" Megan asked remembering all the doors.

Theo shook his head and beckoned Megan to follow him. He opened the door that she'd dismissed as a cupboard and to her complete surprise a flight of stairs was revealed.

"I'll take Tyler whilst you go and take a look."

Megan climbed up the stairs to find herself in a vast white room, with bare floors. A single four-poster bed was pushed up against the far wall. A desk and chair had been placed under the window and when Megan looked out she could see the woodland below. For the first time since she'd seen the wretched dump in the brochure, Megan felt a small ray of hope.

Theo and Tyler had followed behind and her dad now took on the role of estate agent.

"There's more," he said excitedly. "Go through the door!"

Megan did as instructed and found herself in a similar size room, with a sink in the corner and an enormous round window.

"I thought you'd like this room to use as a studio. It has stacks of light and the view of the woods from here are amazing."

"It's great, Dad." Megan smiled for the first time in a very long time. "Thank you."

"We love you just the same as Tyler, Meg," Theo said quietly. "I know it seems like we choose him over you sometimes but that's because he's delicate and we have to take extra special care of him. We don't want to lose him – but we don't want to lose you either. We love you both very much and we want you to be happy."

"I know," Megan replied. She stroked Tyler's hair. "I love him too – more than anything."

Tyler looked at her and smiled, holding his arms out to

her. Megan was his world.

Theo found his wife standing in the kitchen her hands wrapped around a mug of tea. There was a mug of coffee waiting for him.

"Megan's fine," Theo said cheerfully, putting Tyler carefully on the floor, where he started to cry and hold up his arms to be picked up. "I'm not going to carry you all day young man, you're fine where you are."

Cheryl frowned. "So you're going to just let him cry are you?" She put her mug down angrily and picked up Tyler. "Where's Megan now?"

"She's exploring the garden," Theo said. He turned his attention to Tyler. "How is he going to cope with nursery if you…"

"He's not going to nursery," Cheryl snapped, walking over to the kitchen window. "I can't see her."

"Megan's fine." Theo sighed heavily. "Cheryl, we've talked about this; you're going to take charge of the hotel…"

"No, you talked about it," his wife sniped.

"Cheryl, please, this is meant to be a fresh start for us remember?"

She turned and glared at him. "And that means I just forget what you did, Theo? You had an affair, an affair that you brought into our home! That's something you don't forget. You can't expect me to be alright just like that; I need time to try and forgive you." She looked back out of the window. "I don't like us lying to our daughter. She's done so much for her brother, I don't want her resenting him."

"Then why don't you tell her the truth?" Theo asked cautiously.

"Because," Cheryl said softly, "you've already broken my heart. I don't want you breaking hers too."

4. DAISY

Megan walked through the garden at the back of their new home. It had small winding paths that that lead round bare wintry flowerbeds. At the back of the garden were gates, which lead out onto the woodland.

She leaned over it listening to the birds singing and breathing in the smell of damp rotting leaves and wet earth. The terrible screaming of an animal in pain shattered her peace. She turned towards the sound and saw the grass move as something thrashed about in the undergrowth. Without really thinking about what she was doing, she ran through the gate and towards the commotion. She clasped a hand over her mouth in horror as she saw a deer with a metal noose pulled tight around its back foot. The creature looked directly at Megan, its eyes wide with fear. After a moment of calm, it violently pulled against the wire, trying to get away from her.

A soft voice spoke from behind her. "Hush now

darling, it's going to be alright."

Megan turned around to see a girl about the same age but who were several inches shorter.

Megan took a step back. There was something about her that made Megan wary. The girl's blonde hair was cut very short and the right side of her face reminded Megan of a picture of a flower fairy she'd seen in a book about Cicely Mary Barker. The left side of her face was the reason Megan had ashamedly taken a step back; it was an angry mass of scars that looked like they had been caused by a terrible fire.

The mysterious girl walked past Megan, ignoring her obvious repulsion (she was used to the negative reaction by now) and over to the deer. She knelt down and whispered so softly that Megan couldn't hear what was being said. The deer stopped struggling and lay still and the girl rummaged in the bag she'd been carrying, pulling out a small pair of wire cutters.

"You'd be surprised how many times these have come in handy!" she laughed, waving them in Megan's direction.

The girl focused back on the deer, working the cutters to free the deer's foot. It was swollen and bleeding from where the wire had cut deep into the skin. Megan shuddered at the thought of how much pain the poor creature must be feeling but nevertheless it didn't try and get up and run away. The girl held the foot between her badly scarred hands and her lips moved silently. When she let go the swelling had eased and the blood was dry. The deer (seemingly as surprised by the strange events as Megan) got up slowly onto its feet, stared at the girl for a few seconds and then darted off into the trees.

The girl stood up, picking up the wire as she did and held it out for Megan to see.

"Do you know what this is?" she asked.

Megan couldn't respond. She couldn't believe what she'd just seen the girl do. Her brain also refused to stop analysing the girl's scars, despite the small voice inside her head scolding her for being so rude.

"It's called a snare," the girl told her. "Nasty bloody thing; it's used round here for catching rabbits. Megan nodded and the girl continued. "Rabbit comes along and its head goes into the noosey bit. It gets caught and as it struggles, the noose gets tighter and tighter until the poor animal strangles itself. It's not really allowed in these parts so I'm guessing poachers must have put them down."

Megan swallowed hard and then blurted out, "How did you make the deer's foot better?"

"I'm a 'Healer'," the girl said. Seeing Megan's blank

expression, she explained, "All living things have energy which keeps us alive and also helps us heal, I've a little more than most, and with a little bit of magic I can push it through my hands and direct it to who or whatever needs it. It can't make the blind see, or people who are paralysed walk, nothing like you find in the bible, but it can help the healing process. It works best when used alongside medicines, like one of those motors you can put on a pushbike to help you get up steep hills. You still have to peddle but the job is a lot easier."

Did she say with magic? Megan wasn't sure, but she did say that it couldn't cure everything, which probably explained the scars, or maybe there was some rule that you couldn't use your power on yourself. Her eyes flitted back to the scarred side of the girl's face.

"It was a house fire," she replied bluntly.

"Oh," Megan replied.

The girl touched her scars subconsciously. " I survived but my parent's didn't."

"I'm so sorry," Megan said. "I shouldn't have stared. It was rude of me."

"Well, my type of face isn't the sort you see every day is it?" The girl shrugged and took a step towards Megan. "I haven't seen you around here before."

"My name's Megan. My Great Aunt Betty died and my Dad inherited Stone Towers. We moved here because my brother Tyler has really bad asthma. My dad's a doctor and he thinks the country air will be better for his lungs."

"I'm Daisy," the girl said. "Just to warn you, the hotel is haunted. I'm sure most of it is exaggerated for the tourists. Some people love the thought of staying the night in a haunted hotel. No one has ever run out of the building screaming though."

"I don't believe in ghosts," Megan told her.

Daisy looked at her in surprise. "Really?"

"There you are Daisy," a stranger's voice broke their conversation. "I told you not to go wandering off."

Megan turned to see a man with a walking stick staring at her. He was slender and not very tall, with sandy coloured hair peppered with grey. He had a pleasant face with soft lines around his eyes. It took Megan a moment to realise what it was about his eyes that held such attention, both were different colours. The right was a deep warm brown and the left was an icy blue. His eyes weren't the only thing Megan found odd, despite first impressions, when you looked closer, he didn't look particularly old,

"Sorry, Uncle Jack," Daisy replied. "This is Megan. She's just moved into Stone Towers."

Daisy's Uncle Jack smiled pleasantly and held out his hand. "Hello, Megan."

Megan took the hand feeling very shy, and gave it a quick shake.

"I hate to be a kill-joy," Jack said to Megan, "but do your parents know that you're in the woods alone?"

"Erm no," Megan answered, wondering what these two people would think if they knew she'd been used to hopping off a red-double-decker all over London. "I'd better go." She turned to Daisy and waved goodbye. "Bye, Daisy. Nice to meet you."

"Bye, Megan." Daisy smiled.

Jack and Daisy stood in silence watching her leave. Daisy instinctively knew that something wasn't quite right about Megan; she had a gift for such knowledge – like she knew when an animal was hurting, or a plant was thirsty. She could clearly see that Megan had The Glow but she'd said that she didn't believe in ghosts and Daisy knew from her eyes that this was true.

Daisy didn't say anything; she knew Jack would tell her everything when he was ready. Jack was gifted too, he had the ability of Psychometry, meaning that if he touched a person he could see what happened to them in their past. He could also do the same with objects. By touching them, he could tell what happened to whoever owned them. It was all to do with the energy.

"You should be very, very careful using your abilities in front of strangers," Jack said quietly as if Megan would still be able to hear them. "I don't expect to have to tell you that."

"I saw she had The Glow," Daisy replied. "I thought it would be okay, and the deer was hurting so much I couldn't let her suffer any longer."

"Just because someone has an ability doesn't mean they're always open to others having them." Jack gave a small shrug. "It's strange I know, but it does happen."

"Have I put myself in danger?" Daisy looked down the path Megan had taken back to Stone Towers.

"No, because you helped the deer she doesn't think you're bad," Jack replied reassuringly. He placed a comforting hand on Daisy's shoulder and gave her a smile. "She doesn't think you're normal but then I could have simply told her that."

Knowing Jack was teasing, Daisy gave him a gentle thump in the ribs.

"She's the first person I've met with The Glow that doesn't believe in ghosts," she told him.

"She's the only one in her family who has it," Jack

said. "Well, the only one who's alive."

"How on Earth has she gone through life without realising that there are ghosts and spirits around?" Daisy asked.

Jack shrugged. "People see when they want to see," he said. "Sometimes they can't see what they don't understand, or they pass it off as a figment of their imagination, which she does quite a lot." He looked hard at Daisy. "But she's not going to be able to do that for much longer as her ability is growing stronger. Coming here has helped with that."

Daisy nodded. Threshold had an effect on psychic and paranormal abilities, which no doubt attracted supernatural beings as well. Jack once described it like gas to naked flames. Daisy had asked him what would happened if too many 'naked flames' came to Threshold, or one very big one happened to turn up. Jack had looked at her with a strange expression on his face and advised her not to think about it.

"She's going to be different, the type of different she's not used to," Jack said. "She's going to need a friend."

Daisy noticed the way Jack was looking at her.

"What?"

"It will be good for you to have friends who don't have

fur and feathers," Jack replied.

"I have human friends as well," Daisy said.

"Not of your own age," Jack replied. "I don't know anyone her age that is as educated as you: you're the perfect choice."

Daisy stared back at the path. "Gods help her!"

5. RAVENDALE

To just say Megan wasn't happy on her first day of school would be seriously wrong, she was so angry she couldn't put it into words. She thought she'd been more than understanding about moving to a small town and living in place that had been owned by a family member whom she hadn't liked – and that still had her stuff haunting the place. But the last straw in her saintly tolerance was her new school. Her parents had told her it was called Ravendale High School and it was supposed to be very nice, but what had peeved Megan was they hadn't thought that she might like to go and look around the place, or meet her teachers. (Her mood probably wasn't helped by the fact that she phoned Sarah the night before, who after finding out about Megan's new home, talked endlessly about their friends and teachers, which made Megan feel terribly homesick) It all felt rushed and had made Megan feel even more awkward when she found herself standing in her new tutor base with Mrs Barnet standing behind her.

Mrs Barnet was a small, bony looking woman, with a narrow bird-like face, who appeared to be wearing the full colour range of a rainbow, reminding Megan of one of those really annoying children's' television presenters. She ushered Megan to the front of the class "Ladies and gentlemen, may I have you attention for just a moment please," she said loudly, the whole room fell silent, and Megan felt all eyes on her,

"This is Megan's first day at Ravendale and I trust that you're all going to make her feel welcome" she placed her hand gently onto Megan's shoulder. "Why don't you tell us something about yourself."

Megan cringed and desperately tried to find something to say that wouldn't make her sound like a complete fool. "I come from London," Megan said to a captivated audience. At mention of London the rest of the class looked genuinely impressed. Almost every hand shot into the air indicating a question most likely about red buses and Beefeaters, and the Queen. Mrs Barnet ushered their hands down and returned her attention to Megan who she encouraged with a nod of the head to continue. The only thing was that Megan didn't really know what to say. After an embarrassing pause she gushed, "And I like art!"

"I hope you'll bring me some of your work" Mrs Barnet smiled. "Megan you need to sit at that table over there," she instructed pointing towards a table in the far corner of the room. Her table-buddies looked friendly enough, she thought.

After the mortification of meeting her tutor group, Megan made her way to her first lesson, Maths, which was the other side of the rambling school, meaning that she arrived five minutes after everybody else. Thankfully, her Maths teacher took pity on her (did not insist on formal introductions) and guided her to her table with nothing more than a smile and a wave of a hand at the only vacant seat.

As Megan walked past one of the tables, she sensed a girl looking at her intensely. Megan took in the girl's long blond hair tied up in a perfectly neat ponytail held in place with a bow the same blue as her dark blue eyes. Long eyelashes fluttered coyly against her pretty face and the image of an angel sprang into Megan's mind – that was if the girl hadn't had such a nasty smile on her face.

"That's the thickies table," she hissed.

Megan knew she wasn't particularly good at Maths, but just because you found a subject difficult didn't make you 'thick'. Megan took an immediate dislike to the girl. It was clear that she was one nasty piece of work, not that she was going to give her the satisfaction of seeing that she'd got to her. Megan responded with a shrug, placed a sweet smile on her lips and said cutely, "No one is good at everything – not even you!"

The nasty smile turned smug, "Oh but I am!"

"Really?" Megan said sarcastically. "I guess if you're as good at everything as boasting then I must be wrong!"

Someone near the girl tittered, and she turned her head to glare at them. Megan used the opportunity to sit down. Everyone at the table stared at her incredulously.

"You shouldn't have said that to Courtney," a girl whispered. "She's going to make your life hell. She'll make you pay for that."

Megan shrugged and tried her hardest not to look bothered, but she was sure she could feel Courtney's eyes burned into the back of her head. She sighed and heard the voice inside her head ask her why on Earth she couldn't keep her mouth shut.

With the bell for break Megan felt complete relief. All through Maths and the following English class Megan had been bombarded by questions about what it was like to live in London, about her family, her house, her pets, her siblings, etcetera. It had been an endless interrogation making it very hard to concentrate. Now all she just wanted was a break from all the attention. She took her sketchbook form her bag and hustled outside with the hope of finding a quiet place in the playground to sit and draw.

"That's a brilliant picture of a tree," a voice said. "It looks like a photograph."

Megan slammed her book shut. She didn't mind people looking at her artwork if it was going to go on display somewhere, but her sketchbook was private, like a diary, the drawings were how she expressed her thoughts and feelings.

She looked up and found herself looking at a round boy, with thick black hair, and a face that reminded her of a full moon. Kind brown eyes looked out from behind thick-rimmed glasses. He was smiling apologetically.

"Sorry," he said. "If I had known it was private I wouldn't have looked."

Megan went to apologise, she knew she must have seemed grumpy slamming her book like that, she hadn't meant to, she just wanted some quiet time, but before she could explain herself, the boy was shoved roughly from behind,

"That's for laughing at me," Courtney announced. Megan remembered the titter she'd heard come from the back of the classroom.

Standing either side of Courtney, and blocking any teacher's view of what was happening, was two girls. Megan didn't recognise them as being in any of her classes that morning.

"What is your problem?" Megan demanded helping the boy to his feet.

"I don't like ugly, skinny scarecrows," Courtney replied, snatching the sketchbook out of Megan's hand and opening it. She was just about to tear some of the pages out when a pigeon swooped down, and did a very large poop on top of Courtney's head. Distracted by the utter humiliation of it, a scarred hand reached behind her and snatched the sketchbook back off her.

"I'd go and wash that off Courtney," Daisy said as she walked over to Megan and handing back the sketchbook, "the smell will only get worse the longer you leave it." She looked at the boy. "Are you okay, Scott, did you hurt yourself?"

The boy looked pale. "I'm fine thanks," he said quietly.

He took hold of Megan's wrist gently and pulled her close to him, standing in front of her as though to protect her.

"You won't get away with this, Daisy," Courtney hissed. "My Mum's a school governor!"

"Get away with what?" Daisy asked innocently. Two more birds flew overhead and relieved themselves on Courtney's two henchwomen. Screeches of disgust erupted. Daisy wrinkled her nose. "Blimey, what on earth have the local wildlife been eating?"

"You didn't tell us these were Daisy's friends," one of the girls protested.

"I didn't know," Courtney said scowling at Megan and Scott. "Since when does she have friends in this school?"

"I'm not standing here with bird poo on me," Courtney's other friend cried before walking away as quickly as she could.

Courtney's remaining friend took hold of her arm and said, "Come on Courtney let's get this stuff washed off."

Courtney glared at Megan and Scott before allowing herself to be guided away.

"In her case I blame the parents," Daisy said sadly. "They really think the sun shines out of her ass." She looked at Megan and Scott. "I'd best get away from you two before I really damage your reputations."

She turned to leave. Megan realised that she had just stood and stared through all that had happened, and went after Daisy to thank her.

"Wait!" Scott grabbed hold of her hand, which he dropped like a hot coal when she glowered at him. "How do you know Daisy?"

"I met her in the woods the other day," Megan replied. She knew that if she told him about the deer he wouldn't believe her – anyway, there was something about that moment in time that felt almost... sacred. Yes, that was the word; something had run between her and Daisy that was precious and secret.

"That's all?" Scott looked surprised. "She doesn't usually like people so quickly."

"Why's that?"

"She has trust issues. The house fire she was in wasn't an accident," Scott said. Seeing the shocked look on Megan's face he sat down on the bench Megan had been sitting on and continued his story. "Those birds didn't just poo randomly you know, Daisy told them to do it: she's a Witch. So were her Mum and Dad, and they lived in a village not far from here. My Granddad says you can't trust Witches as they're part of nature, and nature is unpredictable. But he also told me that Daisy's parents weren't bad people; they just wanted to show people that their magic could help. Of course lots of people didn't believe that what they were doing was real, it was just tricks, you know like the magicians on the television? But some people did believe. There were those who thought it was great, and then there were people who were afraid. Granddad says that when people are afraid they can become really nasty." Scott stopped to focus on the hole in the knee of his trousers.

Megan's mind was whirling. Scott couldn't leave it there. All at once she felt the overwhelming need to know exactly what happened to Daisy and everything else about her.

"So what happened?" Megan asked impatiently.

Scott snapped off a piece of the frayed cotton and returned to telling his story with the satisfied air of a good storyteller. "Well a couple of teenagers decided they didn't want witches living in their village. They planned to scare them away by setting their house on fire. They said they'd thought the house was empty because there wasn't a car outside. Maybe that was true. Maybe not. Either way they poured petrol through the letterbox and then threw a match in."

Megan gasped and looked across the playground towards where Daisy was crouched down in the dirt. She was drawing something in the ground with a stick.

"Poor Daisy," she said quietly.

"I don't think they would have ever gone to the police station if it hadn't been for Daisy," Scott said. "They said they kept seeing the little girl that had been in the fire. Every time she appeared their hands burnt, and she told them that they would keep burning until they went to the police and faced up to their crime, which is what they did. They weren't sent to prison but to a psychiatric unit somewhere.

"Why was that?" Megan asked.

"Because the people who were looking after Daisy at the hospital said there was no way she could have been visiting them, she was too sick; they must have been sent mad by their guilt was the judges verdict. But you know, I don't think they did imagine it, I think somehow she visited them and that's what really worries me – if she can do something like that when she really badly hurt, what can she do when she's okay. "

"Maybe it's just a story someone made up to scare people and protect Daisy," Megan suggested.

"I don't think so," Scott said sagely. "Look, I'm not trying to scare you, but my Granddad said that the more people who know about these things, the more we can protect ourselves. Everything you thought wasn't real;

fairy-tales, myths, legends, nightmares, they're all real –
even in London! In fact London probably has more places
for them to hide. My Granddad's best friend was taken by a
troll..."

Megan's laughter interrupted Scott's flow. When she
saw the look of hurt on his face she clamped her hand over
her mouth and muttered, "Sorry! I'm sure he *thinks* that's
what happened."

"It did, honest!" Scott said. "When he was our age. No
one believed him; they thought it was his mind playing
tricks on him because he was so upset after he saw a
madman kill his friend.

"Oh, that's terrible," Megan sympathised.

Scott nodded. "My Granddad says he knew what he
saw; he was with him when it happened. That's why he
became an expert on the supernatural and the paranormal.
He says that for some reason Threshold attracts these things
and sometimes they like us to know that they're real. Even
when people in charge, like the police and the **town**
council, try and hide it, it doesn't always work."

The bell rang indicating break-time was over. It was a
harsh sound and it made Scott and Megan jump. Megan
suddenly felt very cold. She wrapped her arms around her
chest and shivered. She wished she could just believe that

Scott was trying to scare her for sport, but she had seen what Daisy had done to the deer's foot – it was nothing short of magical. She looked up at the school; an imposing red-bricked building with a prominent central tower and cupola. Tears pricked her eyes. She wanted to go home. She wanted to go back to London.

6. THE LIBRARY

Megan's first day at Ravendale High went painfully slowly after break. What Scott had said to her kept playing on her mind, making it very hard for her to concentrate. She was certain that everyone thought she wasn't very bright. Courtney, who was unfortunately in most of her classes, didn't say anything more to her, but she did whisper to the others in her class, resulting in Megan getting odd looks for the rest of the day. Scott and his friends were really nice to her, and she tried her best to join in their conversations to distract herself from thinking about how monsters and fairy-tale creatures could actually be real, but thoughts kept making their way through.

By the time she got into the passenger seat of Mum's car she was exhausted.

"How was your day?" Cheryl asked.

"Fine," Megan said wearily.

"Oh for Christ's sake, Megan!" Cheryl snapped. "You're not the only one finding this difficult. Will you stop sulking!"

Megan looked at her Mum shocked and hurt.

"I wasn't sulking," she said. "I'm tired. It was like the first day of term for me today. Not only did I have to try and remember everyone's names and where everything was kept but the teachers teach really differently from the ones back in London and I found it really difficult to keep up." Megan's eyes filled with tears.

Cheryl saw the hurt in her daughter's face and felt like the worst mother in the world. Her own eyes very nearly started to water but she forced them away. Her daughter needed to be comforted and seeing her Mum breaking down was not going to help matters. She gently pulled Megan into a hug.

"I'm so sorry sweetheart," she said softly.

Cheryl rarely lost her temper, unless she was really angry or worried about something. Megan knew that something wasn't right.

"What's wrong Mum?" Megan asked. "Has something happened?"

She pulled away from Cheryl and looked at Tyler who was sitting in his baby seat playing with his toys. He looked fine.

"Nothing's wrong," Cheryl said gently. "I'm just tired

too and there was so much to do today. I didn't know that being an owner of hotel would be so hectic, I thought everything would be left to the manager but no, there are things to approve, and to order; there's accounts, and don't start me on the budget. Then our washing machine decided to have a break-down this morning!" She gave a weak smile. "You remember your Dad said that Aunt Betty had someone to help her do the cleaning in the morning?" Megan nodded. "Her name is Mrs Hodgson – sweet old dear – and she said that Threshold has a really good library." Cheryl smiled; knowing the way to her daughter's heart was a good library. "I was thinking maybe we could go and take a look?"

Megan liked libraries, when she wasn't drawing she was reading, and she knew that this was Mum's way of saying sorry. Megan gave her a smile and nodded.

To get to the library they had to drive through town, which was a treat in itself for Megan. The streets were cobbled and there was a mixture of buildings, from the black and white Tudor buildings, to square Georgian buildings, and Victorian buildings, with patterned bricks and wooden panelling. Most of the buildings that were shops had bay windows made up of little glass panes. The shop signs were wooden with words elegantly painted on them. They passed a bakers which had been made to resemble a gingerbread house; the pharmacy looked like a Medieval apothecary shop, and Megan's favourite, which sold Witchcraft supplies and Pagan artwork, was painted purple and had flowers and leaves decorating the doorway. A huge pentagram hung from the door. Threshold Library looked more like a cathedral than a library. The inside was just as stunning as the outside and Megan couldn't help but mouth the word "wow!" as she gawped, fish-mouthed at the ceiling, thinking that she'd never seen anything quite so beautiful. The high ceiling had been painted to look like a white-clouded sky. Large stained-glass windows played host to images of famous authors and every space was taken up with shelf upon shelf of books – not just modern books, but old leather bound books too.

"Go and have a look round," Cheryl said quietly. "I'll go and get our library cards and then I'll come and find you." Megan looked at Tyler in his pushchair and wondered if she should offer to take him. She'd rather not. She really wanted to go and explore in peace. Mum wrinkled her nose and smiled, "Go on – go and have ten minutes to yourself. He'll be okay with me."

Megan walked off with a spring in her step. She wanted to find the Art section. She looked around for someone who might be able to help her. There were quite a few people browsing, but she didn't want to disturb any of them. Then she saw a woman with a trolley full of books. She was small and round with curly grey hair, a pink cardigan, and glasses perched on the end of her nose. She looked friendly and so Megan walked over to her.

"Excuse me," she said, "where are the books about art?" The woman didn't answer and Megan wondered if she might be deaf, so she spoke a little louder, "Excuse me, where are the books on art?"

"She won't answer you," said a familiar voice. "She's not really there."

Megan jumped and spun round. Daisy stood there, grinning. Instinctively she took several steps away from her.

"Let me guess, Scott told you the story about my burns." Daisy said.

Megan nodded.

"It wasn't me. Whatever some of the village gossips might say."

Megan was confused. Scott had mentioned nothing about people in the village blaming Daisy for the fire. Daisy sensing Megan's discomfort carried on in a hope to reassure her. "My parents had very strict rules about using magic, and number one was never use it to harm others."

Recalling the incident with Courtney in the playground, Megan raised a questioning eyebrow. Daisy shrugged. "Well of course I have off days, especially when they involve that little cow, Courtney, but I'd never do anything that would upset or disappoint Mum and Dad.

"What Scott said was true though, wasn't it?" Megan whispered. "You're a witch – that's how you helped that deer: you used magic on it." Megan looked at Daisy carefully. There was something suspicious about her being here. Then the penny dropped, "That's also how you knew that I'd be here. Why? Are you following me?"

"I'm not *that* weird," Daisy laughed. "I'm here because my Nan's friend works here. Nan has an appointment this afternoon and I couldn't go in with her so I'm hanging out here. To answer your other question, yes I am a Witch, that's with a capital W and we are completely different from the type of witches, which people sometimes believe they are. In the past we were all treated the same way but we're not the same. Witches, real Witches, are linked with nature, and we're able to channel her energy and those of the elements. We can focus on it, then use it for various things."

"Like what, exactly?" Megan asked, wide-eyed and

slightly disbelieving.

"Nothing sinister. Promise. Even though some of our abilities may seem supernatural to some, we can't change people into newts or toads and we can't control a person's thoughts or emotions, nor can our spells do homework, which I've always been disappointed about if I'm honest." Daisy laughed at some secret joke.

"So do you know other Witches?"

"Of course! You'll notice a surprising amount of Witches in the world once you know what you're looking for."

"And what does one look for?" Megan asked with genuine interest.

"Well it's hard to say. We come in all shapes, sizes, colours, apart from green, unless of course, we're not feeling very well and you can get men Witches as well as lady Witches."

"Really?"

Daisy nodded, and leaned in close before whispering, "Just to warn you though, male witches are not called Warlocks, the word Warlock means traitor and you could really upset a male Witch if you called him that."

Megan was surprised at how open Daisy was being about the whole Witch thing. 'Surely', she thought, 'there must be some code of secrecy or something?' "Okay," Megan said quietly hoping she wouldn't have to remember everything Daisy had just said. She looked at the woman, who was now behind Megan and nodded. "She's a Residual."

Megan looked back in the given direction. "A what?"

"She died about four years ago," Daisy said.

"She's a ghost?"

"No, not exactly – watch what she's doing."

Megan watched as the woman picked up the books from the trolley, but as soon as they touched the shelf they disappeared.

"The same books over and over again," Daisy said. "Maureen loved this library, and when people have strong feelings about a place, they leave a little piece of themselves there in the form of residual energy. Sometimes people mistake them for ghosts or spirits because you can walk through them."

"Why doesn't someone get rid of it?" Megan asked quietly.

"Because most people can't see it and it's not hurting anyone," Daisy said.

"Why can we see it?" Megan asked, wishing she were one of the 'most people'

"I don't know, maybe we're on the right frequency or something, you know like mobile phones? Some people find that their phones can pick up on a network whilst others in the same place can't?" Daisy shrugged. She walked over to Maureen and reached out letting her fingers go through the woman's arm. "Not everything that's different is dangerous, or scary." she glanced back. "The art books are three aisles down, on your right."

"Thanks," Megan replied smiling.

She headed off towards the art books but stopped; *'not everything that's different is dangerous or scary.'* The words had sunk in deep making her think – Daisy couldn't have been the only one on the playground who saw what Courtney was doing but she had been the only one who had gone over and helped. She turned to see Daisy with her fingertips in the Residual's arm.

"What are you doing?" Megan asked, slightly alarmed.

"Sorry, I thought you'd gone," Daisy said. "You know you turn the television off you get that static on the screen sometimes?" Megan nodded, "that's what a Residual feels like, it makes your fingers tingle, come and have a try."

"I don't want to," Megan replied. "And could you not do that, it looks creepy."

Daisy looked disappointed as she took her fingers out

of the Residual's arm. "Did you forget something?" she asked.

"I wanted to say thanks for coming over and helping me and Scott today," Megan said.

"You can repay me by doing it for someone else one day," Daisy replied.

It was at this point Tyler came toddling over and wrapped his arms around Megan's leg.

"Oh, look at you," Daisy said softly, "aren't you a little diamond?"

Tyler peeked round Megan's legs, and she braced herself for crying, tears, and people staring. Tyler giggled.

"Lights," he said pointing at Daisy. "Pre-tty."

He walked over to Daisy and moved his hands around her as though catching bubbles. Whatever it was he could see, Megan couldn't. Daisy crouched down so that she was the same height as him and wiggled her fingers and Tyler laughed as though it was the funniest thing he had ever seen.

"Hello," Cheryl said, standing next to Megan with the pushchair.

Megan saw that her Mum was looking at Daisy with an expression she hadn't seen before. It made her mum look unfamiliar. Megan remembered how she too had stared when she had seen Daisy's scars and felt horribly ashamed.

"This is my friend Daisy," Megan said.

Cheryl looked at the girl in front of her. She wished her first reaction were to look pleased that Megan had found someone she would call a friend, instead it was pity – a terrible sadness that something awful had happened to the child. She knew that her expression was betraying her and her guilt was almost sickening. Embarrassment clawed at her stomach as Tyler placed his hands on the girl's blemished skin.

"Well, hello, Daisy. It's nice to meet you," she said resisting the urge to pull Tyler away, "I'm Cheryl: Megan's mum."

Daisy looked up at her and smiled, gently pulling Tyler's hands away before guiding the little boy back towards his Mum. "I think Mummy needs a cuddle," she said.

Tyler beamed at his Mum who hugged him before placing him into the pushchair. Someone called Daisy's name and Megan and Cheryl looked to see a woman standing near the library's entrance. Megan wasn't sure if you could get elderly angels but if you did, she was certain they'd look like this. She was tall and willowy with a delicate elfin face, framed by long white hair.

"That's my Nan," Daisy said. "See you at school tomorrow, Megan."

"Bye, Daisy."

Daisy walked away with her hands in her cardigan pockets.

"I stared too when I met her," Megan told Cheryl quietly. "She said her type of face wasn't the sort you see every day, so I think she's used to it."

"Why doesn't she wear a mask or something?" Cheryl murmured, thinking out loud.

"Mum!" Megan protested. "I can't believe you just said that, especially when you and Dad always say that it doesn't matter what someone looks like, it's who they are that's important."

"It is," Cheryl agreed, "but it might make people stop staring at her."

"Actually," Megan responded irritably, "I think it would make people stare at her even more because they'd be wondering what she's hiding." Megan frowned. "A girl at school was going to rip up my sketchbook today and Daisy stopped her."

"Who was this girl?" Cheryl asked immediately defensive of her little girl.

"That doesn't matter, what does matter is that even

though she doesn't know me very well Daisy came and helped me," Megan replied. "That's the type of person she is, Mum, and that's what's important, not what she looks like."

Cheryl muttered something inaudible under her breath, which Megan chose to hear as an apology, although she wasn't quite done yet. "And just to let you know, the reason she looks like she does is because she was in a house fire that killed her Mum and Dad! Every time someone asks her what happened she gets reminded of that, but she doesn't seem at all sorry for herself, and I think that makes her very brave."

With that, Megan pushed Tyler towards the books on art, leaving Cheryl wondering when her daughter had grown up so much.

7. MEGAN'S FIRST GHOST

It seemed to Megan that each day was like the last, what many people would consider boring. During the week, she would go to school, do her lessons, go home, paint or draw and do her homework. At the weekends, she'd play with Tyler, finish off any homework she had left, and if the weather were fine, she would go and play in the garden. Every two weeks Megan would call Sarah to find out what she was doing and what was going on in London, but even after nearly a month at Threshold she was beginning to find that she and her old friend were starting to grow apart. Sarah had made friends with someone called Sophie, and she had started going round her house after school and going to Karate with her, and dance classes; two things Megan had no real interest in. It was beginning to get hard to find something to talk about. Everyday her Mum, or Dad, (who was now working at St. Pantaleon Hospital, in the center of Threshold) dropped her off outside the school, mostly parking by *The Woman* who stood by the oak tree.

She wasn't always there, and at first Megan thought it was just her eyes playing tricks on her. But after several days of seeing her in the same place, always in the same impossibly eerie posture (it looked like someone had twisted her head all the way round and had left it at a funny angle,) and in the same outfit, (a grey suit covered with blood) she guessed *The Woman* must be a Residual. She remembered how Daisy had said that Residuals were made when someone had strong feelings about a place, and looking at her, Megan guessed that whatever had caused her death had caused some very strong feelings.

Megan tried to ignore her as much as she could. There was something about the figure that felt wrong – maybe even a little bit sinister. Every time she walked past *The Woman,* her blood ran ice cold. On the first day she had glanced up into the woman's tragically mangled face – it was so disgusting that it nearly made her sick. She resolved not to look on it again, which is why she failed to notice that every time *The Woman* saw Megan, she cracked a spidery smile.

"What rhymes with bound?" April asked. April was one of Scott's friends; she had, rosy cheeks, and warm brown eyes. Megan liked her. They were doing poetry in

English.

"Frowned, gowned, ground, mound, pound," Megan offered.

"You do know poems don't always have to rhyme?" Tim said to April firmly, although not unkindly. Tim was short, with ears that stuck out and glasses that made his eyes look huge. Megan could never quite shake away the image of a wood mouse.

"I know," she rolled her eyes, "but I'm writing a funny one," April replied. "I always think funny poems always sound better if they rhyme."

The boy next to Tim (still nameless to Megan even after several shared lunches) burst into life, reciting, "Mary had a little lamb; its fleece was white and wispy. Then it caught foot and mouth, and now it's black and crispy."

"Ben!" Ms Chadwick called across the classroom. "I hope that's not an example of your contribution to this exercise."

"No Miss," Ben replied meekly.

Megan put her hand up. " Ms Chadwick could I please go to the toilet?" she asked.

"It's only half an hour until break, Megan, can't you wait?" she asked. Megan shook her head. "Okay but be quick, I'm about to introduce a new task"

Megan made her way to the nearest toilets. When she was finished, she washed her hands, and tried to tidy her hair in the mirror. It looked even more wild than usual, as though she'd been mildly electrocuted. The more she patted it down, the more it wanted to stand up.

"You really should buy a good Silicone cream," a voice said from behind her. "You put it all over your hair when it's damp, and then comb it straight. That's the only way you're going to tame those locks."

Megan mouth went dry. She hadn't heard the toilet door go, and the voice came from right behind her, almost at her ear, meaning she should have been able to see whoever it was reflected in the mirror, but there was nothing. She turned slowly with the hope of being able to make a dash for the door. She found herself looking right into the eyes of *The Woman,* and she was smiling.

"I knew you could see me," she said sounding pleased. "I need you to listen carefully, there's something I need you to do."

Megan didn't want to do anything for this woman.

"Are you paying attention?" the woman demanded.

"Oi!" a voice protested, and to Megan's horror a girl walked through the wall. "Leave the poor kid alone, she obviously came in here for a reason and it wasn't to speak to you."

The girl was taller than Megan, and her face reminded her of a Siamese cat. She was slender, with long limbs, and dressed completely in black. Her shoulder-length hair was a deep, shocking red that seemed to flare like fire as she glared angrily at the woman.

"I let her finish," the woman responded, folding her arms defiantly. "And I was here first so wait your turn!"

"I'm not here for her help, love," the young woman replied lighting a cigarette. "Shame on you, picking on a kid – I'll take you to someone who is older if you're that desperate."

"It needs to be her," *The Woman* snapped. "Who are you to stop me?"

The girl blew smoke into her face. "Would you like to find out?"

Megan had no desire to know. She turned and ran.

"Are you okay?" April asked when Megan came back to the classroom. "You don't look very well."

"You're shaking," Tim frowned.

"I'm just feeling a little bit sick," Megan replied, which was true. "I'll be okay."

She knew she couldn't tell them what she'd just seen. The classroom door had a large window in it, and Megan could see *the woman* standing there, haunting her. She wasn't alone; Megan's strange guardian was there too. She wished she could go over to Scott's table and talk to him, but she knew the other children would listen in, and the last thing she wanted was for everyone to think she was crazy.

As soon as everything was tided away for break, the other children started filing out the room oblivious to the two dead people standing at the door. Megan tried to think of an escape so that she could get to Scott and find somewhere private to talk. Before she realised what was happening, Scott grabbed her arm and quickly pulled her into the furthest corner of the room. Megan wondered why she hadn't thought of that.

"What's wrong?" he asked quietly. "Tim and April said you were upset about something."

Megan wasn't sure how he could help but as her Gran always said, a problem shared is a problem halved.

"I have two ghosts following me," Megan whispered, knowing full well that she sounded completely mental. "They were in the girls' toilets, and they're now waiting for me outside the door." Scott stared at her silently, and she felt her stomach clench. "You don't believe me do you?"

Scott nodded slowly, "Yes, I believe you. I was born in Threshold remember? I'm just trying to think if my

Granddad has told me anything that might help."

"Come on you two it's break time," Ms Chadwick called from her desk. "I think one of you has Daisy waiting for you."

Daisy was leant against the doorframe with her hands in her pockets. The ghosts had moved on but Megan had a strong feeling that they weren't that far away. She took a deep breath and walked over to her, pleased that Scott was following her even though he was little nervous about Daisy. They made their way quickly into the empty cloakroom.

"What's happened?" Daisy asked gently clearly concerned.

"How did you know something is wrong?" Scott replied.

"I can pick up on what people are feeling," Daisy explained. "In places like this it's buzzing, but I learn to block them out, a bit like have the television on when you're doing your homework, but sometimes something catches your attention. Fear can be pretty loud, it's not that hard to find out where it's coming from." She looked pointedly at Megan. "Care to share?"

Megan had been right, the ghosts had moved a little away as though they weren't trying to listen into their conversation, but they wanted to be close in case they were going to be called over.

Megan whispered in surprise, "You can't see them? There are two ghosts over by the Shakespeare display."

"No," Daisy said, "I'm afraid ghosts and spirits are different from residuals."

"There's a girl who is smoking," Megan replied, "and a woman who looks like she's been in a really horrible accident. She's gross."

"See," the girl said to the woman viciously, "I told you were in a right mess."

"Why didn't anyone tell me?" the woman asked looking horrified.

The girl shrugged. "Maybe they didn't think it was polite."

Ms Chadwick picked up her books before leaving for the staff room. "Come on you three." Ms Chadwick said, sighing. "Outside."

The three of them headed out, Megan feeling much safer in numbers. Once outside Daisy took Megan and Scott to her usual place under the tree where she told them to sit down. Then she drew a large circle around them, muttering something under her breath; she stepped inside the circle and took a small pouch from her pocket, sprinkling what looked like dried leaves around them.

"Okay," Daisy said sitting down, "I've done a spell so we won't get interrupted by the ghosts and I threw in a little something so we appear very uninteresting to everyone around us, so we won't have any eavesdroppers."

"Two spells at the same time," the girl appeared next to Scott smoking another cigarette. Megan felt a fleeting concern for the girl's health but then realised how silly such a concern was. "That's pretty powerful stuff, she's a Witch you definitely want on your side."

"The girl has managed to get in," Megan told Daisy.

"Then she must be a spirit," Daisy said. "She wouldn't have got in otherwise.'

"I thought ghosts and spirits were the same thing," Scott said confused.

"Well kind of – both are souls," Daisy replied "but a spirit is a soul which has gone to Heaven or whatever you want call it, and a ghost is a soul who is for reason or other is stuck here on Earth."

"How do they get stuck on Earth?" Megan asked.

"Lots of reasons," Daisy said. "It can be because they don't want to leave their family and friends behind or they're afraid of what might be waiting for them on the other side, or they have something they have to finish before they go."

Megan looked at the girl and asked her directly, "Why are you and that woman bothering me?"

"Bothering you?" she cackled a rough laugh, "I'm not 'bothering' you, I'm your spirit guide!" the girl replied. Megan had no idea what the girl was talking about. "Everyone has a Spirit Guide," she went on, "yet most people don't know that we're there; we're usually that 'gut feeling' that tells you whether something is or isn't a good idea."

Megan wondered if that's why she had run to investigate the hurt deer. Normally she would have gone to get her parents; she wouldn't have go running in blindly into a situation. It made sense that someone was guiding her.

"My name's Tabitha."

"And you died because you smoked cigarettes?" Megan asked.

"The adverts are true." Tabitha shrugged and raised her eyebrows.

"But you look like you're only about eighteen how many did you smoke?"

"I was seventeen when I died. I started when I was seven." Tabitha replied. Megan's mouth fell open unattractively.

"My Mum thought it looked cute. She used to dress me all Shirley Temple. It was the only way she paid me any attention," she smiled sadly. "Yeah, I guess she was never going to win any mothering awards. To answer your other question, I saw how much Lauren, that's the woman's name, scared you and to stop her, she needed to think I was a fellow ghost. Because I manifested, it meant you could see me too."

"And why can I see both of you?" Megan asked.

"Because you've got The Glow," Daisy said quietly. Megan looked at her and raised a quizzical eyebrow. Daisy continued, "It's the ability to be able to see ghosts and spirits, it's called The Glow because the people who have it give off a soft light, it attracts ghosts and spirits."

"Oh wow!" Scott gasped looking impressed.

"How do you know I've got The Glow?" Megan asked Daisy.

"I can see it," Daisy told her.

"And you didn't say anything?" Megan frowned. "You could have warned me, I thought you were my friend."

"What could I have said?" Daisy asked. "Hey, I'm Daisy, a Witch, do you know you've got the ability to see ghosts and spirits, only you obviously don't know it yet. Be honest would you have believed me?"

"No, but…"

"So I've stuck around until you needed me," Daisy said. "From experience that's what friends do."

"Believe me, Megan," Tabitha told her gently, "you've got a good one there."

"Is there any way I can get rid of it?" Megan asked Daisy ignoring Tabitha. "Do you know any spells or potions that will make it go away?"

"You can't make it go away," Daisy said. "You can tell yourself that you don't see anything, like when you're little and you tell yourself that you don't really need a dummy and eventually you don't need it anymore. You can train your brain not to see ghosts, and because you don't respond to them they'll stop bothering you."

Megan looked towards Tabitha and asked, "And you can take them to someone who can really help them? That's what you said to that woman, Lauren. You said that I was too young."

Before Tabitha could answer, Scott butted in, "But she must have come to you for a reason. She must have thought…"

"Well she thought wrong," Megan said sharply. "I don't want to…" she ran out of steam – she wasn't even sure what it was that she was being asked to do.

Daisy took her by the hand and said calmly, "But it's a chance to help someone. Okay maybe not this time, but you haven't learnt how to use your ability yet. New things are always scary. But imagine when you're older and regretting throwing your gift away."

"I don't think I'll regret not using something I never even knew I had," Megan replied. "I just want to be normal." She stood up. "I want a normal, boring life, with no ghosts, no spirits, just a job hopefully doing something with art, a house, and a cat. I don't want people staring at me and whispering that I'm different, that I'm weird like they do with you, Daisy. I'm not strong enough." Megan felt tears stinging her eyes. "I'm just not."

Scott stared at her with his mouth slightly open, and Megan realised with a blush that she had just called her friend weird. Daisy was looking blankly at the ground and Megan found that more upsetting than if she had looked upset or angry. Megan turned and walked through the circle, not seeing her friend wince.

The ghost-woman, Lauren, appeared next to Megan as soon as she walked onto the playground. She looked much better, her suit was no longer covered in blood, and her face was now unmarked. Megan thought that the way her dark wavy hair framed her face made her look quite beautiful, but even though the woman's head was back on straight and she no longer looked like a car-crash victim, Megan still looked away. If she was going to convince herself that ghosts didn't exist then it was going to start right now.

"Where did you go?" Lauren asked. Megan put her head down and carried on walking. "Excuse me, I'm talking to you! I really need your help."

The bell rang indicating the end of break time and Megan filed back into the school building with the rest of the children. She felt her heart clench when ghostly fingers passed through her arm.

"Please," Lauren whispered, "don't ignore me."

Megan gritted her teeth. Ignoring her was exactly what she was going to do.

8. THE MONROES

It wasn't until halfway through Maths that Lauren decided to leave Megan alone. She allowed herself a smile of relief, at last able to concentrate on her work, well, that was until Scott slid into the empty chair next to her. Whenever one of the children from the higher Maths tables finished they were allowed to go and help those on the lower tables.

Megan looked at him. "Are you going to tell me how selfish I'm being?" she asked.

Scott shook his head. "It's your choice what you do with your ability and I'll be your friend no matter what you decide," he said quietly. "You hurt Daisy, it was an accident but it still hurt.

Megan nodded. A blush of shame crept over her cheeks. "I should have told her she wasn't weird. I really didn't mean to be horrible it's just..."

"No," Scott shook his head, "I don't think you quite

understand. Sure the whole *wanting to be normal* speech may have hurt her feelings but that wasn't what hurt her. You know that spell she did?" Megan nodded. "It made a sort of bubble around us, and that bubble needed to be made from energy; it was her energy that made it, and it was attached to her." Megan frowned, not quite understanding where Scott was going. "When you walked away, she didn't have a chance to make a doorway for you, so you tore straight through her energy. Daisy explained it better than me, but I could tell it hurt her, it hurt her a lot. She looked really sick and her nose started bleeding."

Megan's stomach twisted into knots. "Is she going to be okay?"

"I've just seen her from the window," Scott said. "Her Nan was picking her up. I don't think she's ever had time off since starting here."

Megan felt awful – she'd hurt her friend deeply, (alright she hadn't done it on purpose) but the whole reason Daisy had done the spell in the first place was to help her. She looked at Scott and asked, "Do you know where she lives?"

Scott shook his head, and Megan felt her heart sink with disappointment. Then an idea came to her, she couldn't believe after all her protests that she had even thought of it, but she had done something terrible and needed to make it right, and she knew someone could help her. She just wasn't sure how to go about it.

"You've just got to think about me," Tabitha's voice replied to her silent question. "But after what you said earlier, I'm a little surprised."

Megan swallowed hard. "I'm really sorry," she said whispered. "I've done something really bad."

Daisy Monroe lived in a small thatched cottage called Cobwebs. It was a pretty little building with white walls, and red painted windowpanes and doors. It stood on the outskirts of town, and backed onto the woods where she and Megan had first met.

"She's got a long way to walk to school hasn't she?" Cheryl said as she parked her car outside the cottage.

Cheryl had agreed to drive her here in order to stop her daughter's sobs. Megan had kept them bottled in all day, but the familiar and loving sight of her mother released them. No matter what soothing words she had offered, Cheryl hadn't been able to calm her down. All she could do was pull her into a hug, and gently rub her back until Megan had managed to catch her breath.

"Who's upset you darling?" she asked gently,

remembering that only yesterday Megan had mentioned a girl who had tried to rip up her sketchbook. She suspected that this girl had now done something else.

"I've really hurt Daisy, Mum." Megan confessed. "I-I said some things I shouldn't have, and then she went home ill."

"And you think what you said upset her so much it made her ill?" Cheryl couldn't believe her daughter would be capable of anything like that.

"Mum I need to go and say that I'm sorry." Megan pulled out a piece of paper onto which she had written down Daisy's address. "Please, will you drive me there?"

Cheryl nodded, proud that her daughter had grown into such a fine young lady. "Of course, sweetie."

"Would you like me to come in with you?" Cheryl asked.

Megan nodded; she knew that she should really do it alone but she didn't want to be turned away and if she got stuck with her words maybe Mum would be able to help her out.

The door was opened by Daisy's Nan. She didn't look angry but smiled pleasantly first at Megan and then at Cheryl who was holding the cute-card, Tyler.

"Hello, I'm Megan, Daisy's friend. I've come by

because I need to see Daisy."

Daisy's Nan looked at her suspiciously. "Well, I'm very sorry but Daisy isn't really well enough to socialise at the minute.

Megan shuffled on the spot and cleared her throat. "I think that might be something to do with me; I said something really bad and I upset her. Could I come in and apologise to her please?" The words came out as a rush, and Megan was worried that she would have to say it all again, or she would have to explain exactly what it was she had said.

"Daisy didn't tell me why she's upset," Daisy's Nan said. "I thought it was because it was because she was feeling ill. She doesn't like missing school; she's always afraid that she'll miss something important. I guess that you'd better come in." She stood to one side and waved them in. "She's feeding her Granddad at the moment but you're welcome to go and talk to her."

Daisy's Nan held out a hand to Cheryl and introduced herself, "Hello I'm Una," she said pleasantly.

"I'm Cheryl," Cheryl replied. "And this is Tyler."

Megan glanced down the hallway and took in the quirky surroundings. It was one of the strangest interior design jobs that Megan had ever seen. Instead of wallpaper, someone had painted a woodland mural on the walls, and there was a thick green carpet on the floor. Megan knew that her mother would be fretting about the cleaning implications and she smiled wryly to herself.

"Patrick's room is down there on the left," Una told Megan as she took their coats. "There are two things I must warn you about before you go in. My husband has something called dementia – have you heard of it?" Megan shook her head. "He gets very confused and forgetful, which makes him frightened sometimes, so if he starts shouting, don't take it personally. The other thing you should know is last year he had a stroke."

"I've heard of those," Megan said.

"It's left him paralysed down the left side and blind." Una said. She cast a look at Cheryl who was weighing up whether she should suggest Megan come back another day.

"Shall we have some tea whilst the girls chat?" Una asked.

Megan didn't wait to hear her Mum's answer; she'd already gone and knocked on Patrick's door.

Megan had expected to see a sick, old man, dribbling and smelling of wee, his body twisted because of the stroke but when she opened the door, she saw a handsome elderly man even though the left side of his face had dropped to

78

one side, and his arm was curled up against his chest. He was sat up in bed, with a tea towel acting as a bib to protect his pyjamas. Everything in the room was bright and cheerful. An old fashioned record player turned in the corner of the room sending out some old crooner number. Brightly coloured flowers were placed in vases around the room; their scent added to the smell of rich soap and spiced aftershave.

Daisy didn't turn to look at Megan but continued to carefully spoon food into Patrick's mouth. Jack, who was sitting next to the bed stood up and gestured for Megan to sit down.

"I'll go and see if there's any tea on the go." Jack said, excusing himself.

Megan sat down and looked at Daisy; her skin was grey and there were dark shadows around her dulled eyes.

"Don't feel guilty," Daisy said softly. "You weren't to know what was going to happen."

"Who is this, Brenda?" Patrick asked reaching out his good hand towards Daisy.

"This is Megan, Grandpa," Daisy replied taking hold of the hand and placing it to the unscarred side of her face. "She's a friend from school."

"Hello," Megan said.

Daisy picked up the spoon she was using to feed Patrick. "You need to eat just a little bit more," she said.

Patrick smiled, and with his face dropping the way it was, it looked strange. "Are you looking after me again, Brenda?" he said. "You're going to make someone a wonderful wife one day."

Megan saw how Daisy swallowed hard when he said this. She cleared her throat and put the spoon to his tightly shut lips.

"Please," she said quietly, "just a few more."

Patrick shook his head and closed his eyes. A few seconds later he was snoring.

Daisy gently took the tea towel from around his neck and used it to wipe away the food away from around his mouth, he didn't wake.

"He thinks I'm my Mum," Daisy explained. "When I tried to explain to him once I was his granddaughter and Mum was dead, it was like he was hearing the news for the very first time. It was terrible; it took him hours to calm down."

Megan didn't know what to say. Suddenly every word and phrase seemed inadequate.

Daisy got up slowly and walked stiffly towards the door. "Come on, let's go to my room where we can talk."

Megan studied Daisy carefully, acutely aware that she was responsible for her friend's injuries.

If a bookshop, a Kew Gardens' greenhouse and a Victorian curiosity shop were mixed together and plonked into a reasonable size area of a cottage, you'd get Daisy's bedroom. Megan thought it was amazing.

Daisy sat down on her bed and smiled when Megan sat down next to her.

"I'm really sorry about what I said," Megan said contritely. "You're not weird. I'm really sorry that I hurt you."

"You didn't mean to." Daisy shrugged. "And compared to most people I am pretty weird," she laughed. "Actually, even compared to other Witches, I'm not completely normal." A small smile came to Daisy's lips. "From what I hear, normal is seriously overrated."

Megan wasn't sure about that but she didn't want to upset Daisy any more, instead she took a deep breath and said, "I thought about what Scott said about Lauren coming to me for a reason. I want to help her but I don't want to do it on my own." Megan sought out Daisy's eyes. "I know I've got my guide Tabitha but I need someone who everyone can see, otherwise they'll think that I'm completely crazy. I know Scott has some knowledge about these things but you… you understand them."

Daisy was quiet. She was thinking things over. It made Megan nervous to think that she might need to take such serious consideration. When Daisy finally offered her a smile it was with much relief.

"Nan said I'm having tomorrow off school, and believe me there's no way I can make her change her mind, but I'll be back the next day so don't worry; you're not going to have to do this on your own."

Megan wasn't sure how to articulate the heartfelt gratitude she felt for her friend so she did the only thing she could think of and pulled Daisy into a tight, giggly hug.

Daisy found it very hard to keep her eyes open during dinner; when she nearly landed face down into her mash potato, Una gently suggested that she go to bed. Daisy didn't need much persuading. When she got into bed she fell asleep as soon as her head hit the pillow.

Jack cleared up the dinner things, whilst Una went and gave Patrick his evening drink. A large dog trotted through the kitchen. With his huge bat like ears and his long fur that looked like it had been dragged through a bush, he made a good impression of a floor mop. He carried one of Daisy's shoes in his mouth and he sat down on the floor wagging his tail madly. Jack smiled and went to reclaim the shoe but the dog jumped to his feet and gave a small muffled woof whilst stepping back and, wagging his tail harder.

"Albie," he said softly, "come on mate, not tonight!" He took hold of the shoe and gave it a firm pull. Albie let go. "Good boy!"

Una came back into the kitchen and looked at the shoe Jack was holding. "Where on earth did that come from?"

"Albie brought it to me."

Una stopped in her tracks. "Where is he now?"

"Plonked himself in front of the fire on your best Afghan rug," Jack replied.

The kitchen was the largest room in the cottage; it had an impressive Aga and substantial country furniture made from rough looking wood. Pots and pans hung from the ceiling along with drying herbs giving the impression of industry and efficiency. Either side of the open fire were two comfortable chairs and in front of it was the rug – the one where Albie was sitting, only Una knew before she even looked that she wouldn't be able to see him (she didn't have The Glow or Jack's affliction) Albie had been dead twelve years. It was one of the only times in their long and happy marriage that Una had seen Patrick cry; Albie and Patrick had been inseparable until death had cruelly split them apart. Una knew exactly why Albie had come home to visit and she asked in a quiet tremulous voice, "How long do we have left with him?"

"I don't know, Una. I'm so sorry, I..."

"You've done everything you possibly could," Una cleared her throat. "I've never been very good at saying goodbyes."

Jack returned his gaze to the fire wishing he could say something to make it at least a little easier.

9. LAUREN

Lauren was so relieved that Megan had agreed to finally listen to her that she didn't let herself be angry about Megan's initial rudeness. Tabitha explained to Lauren how Megan had only just discovered her gift and that she needed to be patient. Lauren had shrugged her shoulders and replied, "I've waited this long, one more day won't hurt."

When Tabitha had reported back from her meeting with Lauren, Megan found herself feeling terribly guilty; she wondered just how long Lauren had been waiting for someone who could help her. Tabitha had arranged for them all (Scott and Daisy included) to meet with Lauren at break the next day; the day that Daisy was due to return to school.

The next morning, Daisy walked in to school looking tired, but not as ill. Scott who was in the same Chemistry class as her, informed her about the break time meeting and said that Megan had asked if she'd mind coming along.

This whole Glow stuff was still a little scary and Megan wanted the morale support. They'd agreed to meet at the picnic table near the nature garden; a place always quiet. Lauren was waiting for them.

They didn't waste time on chitchat and Lauren was keen to get on with their conversation, "I need you to give a message to my husband Mr. Gibb," she said.

Megan screwed her forehead in surprise. "Mr Gibb that works here?"

Lauren nodded.

Mr. Gibb was one of the school's Biology teachers; a thin man, he had a weasel-like face, and thin brown hair, which was slowly getting thinner at the front. He was quiet and patient, and very rarely smiled and never told a joke.

Megan turned to her friends and relayed the information that Lauren was Mr Gibbs wife.

"She died in an accident three years ago," Scott said. "Why does she want to talk to him now?"

"Well, this is the first time she's probably had a chance to," Megan reminded him. "You know about what happened to her then?"

Lauren sat tapping her fingers nervously on her leg waiting for Megan to finish.

Scott nodded. "Mostly from the usual gossip you get

around school," he said. "She died when her convertible went out of control and flipped over; she broke her neck."

Lauren winced on hearing of her own tragic end and Megan felt a moment of social awkwardness. Lauren's voice was thick with emotion when she spoke, "It wasn't quite like that."

Tabitha exhaled a long plume of smoke and shot Lauren a warning glance. "Ssh! They're children, they don't need to know all the gruesome details."

Lauren let out a deep sigh, rolled her eyes and sniped, "That's exactly why I don't think you should be doing that in front of them!"

"Only one of them can see me," Tabitha snapped. "And the other two aren't even affected by it, look!" She blew smoke in Daisy's face. "Besides I'm not exactly a walking advertisement for smoking." Tabitha waved her hand mockingly, "Hello, dead teenager here!"

Daisy, oblivious to the bickering going on around her and the smoke which had blown in her face, grimaced and said, "Sounds painful."

Megan returned her attention to Lauren. "What do you want me to say to him?" Megan asked.

"The day I died we'd had an argument," Lauren said. "I wanted to go to a party and Tom said that he had to stay late after school to help some children with a project but that he would meet me there afterwards. He loves being a teacher and I know he loved me but I was having such a bad week and I was tired, and angry. God, I felt bad about myself, and I wanted him to feel bad too for some stupid reason. Maybe it was jealousy: I said he was putting his students before me and he said that wasn't true but it didn't feel like it. I knew that marrying a teacher is a bit like marrying the job; he couldn't always leave on time and the marking ate into our weekends, and... I was so stupid..." She raised the back of her hand to wipe away a tear. Megan found herself thinking how curious it was; she'd never thought that a dead person could cry, come to think of it she didn't think a dead person could hold a conversation. "I said maybe I shouldn't have married a teacher. It was a horrible thing to say. He had to go to work and so it was left hanging. When I'd calmed down and realised what a nightmare I'd been I thought I could apologise properly when he got home. I had an interview that afternoon so I was probably preoccupied. I was half way there when I noticed I'd left my wedding ring behind. It was loose and I'd taken it off when I'd been cleaning. I put it on the mantelpiece so as not to lose it. I was thinking about going back for it when there must have been some oil or something on the road because the car started to skid and then it flipped. Next thing I knew I was standing by the side of the road, watching people screaming and running towards the car..." Lauren stopped to swallow down her crying. "I went home to wait for Tom. I wanted him to know that I was sorry. When he came home he couldn't hear me. He found my wedding ring where I left it."

Megan repeated to her friends what Lauren had told her.

Daisy, quick as ever said, "So for three years Mr. Gibb thought his wife didn't want to be married to him anymore?"

Lauren nodded and Megan copied her.

"That explains a lot of things," Scott said. "My sister had him as a teacher before I started here and she said he was brilliant."

"He still is." Lauren frowned.

"Lauren still thinks he is," Megan told him.

"Yeah he's nice," Scott said, "but before his wife died, when he taught you something you could get it straight away, he was good at explaining things, and most of the time you didn't notice you were learning important stuff. He was funny, okay, not as funny as Mr. Suns who teaches Physics but you could have a laugh with him; he ran science clubs, and the choir, and he played the guitar, he doesn't do anything like that anymore. It's as though he likes being here but he just doesn't love it."

Megan sighed; she felt sorry for Mr. Gibb she really did but how on earth was she going to go up to a man she really didn't know, tell him that his wife was a ghost, and she wanted to tell him that she hadn't been leaving him. Megan thought what she would do if someone came up to her and told her that a dead loved one wanted to pass on a message.

"How am I going to do this?" she asked. "How am I going to get Mr. Gibb to believe me?"

"Lauren will tell you something that only she and Mr. Gibb will know," Tabitha said.

Lauren nodded with a cheeky smile, "I can think of a few."

"One that's appropriate!" Tabitha added, giving Lauren a look.

Megan relayed the plan. "It'll probably be best to do it after school," Daisy said. "After getting him to believe that his wife is still around in spirit form, his mind isn't going to be on teaching – he'll probably need to go and lie down, or something."

"My Dad is picking me up after school," Scott said. "I

really can't be late; he's very busy. If I'm not out right away he'll have to go." He noticed Daisy's sympathetic look. "He is coming today, he promised. He really means it this time. I'm sorry, Megan, I wish I could help."

Megan turned her attention to Daisy. "Okay, we'll meet outside Mr. Gibb's classroom after school."

All she had to worry about for now was how to get through the rest of the school day.

10. MR GIBBS

Megan stood outside Mr. Gibb's classroom feeling sick with nerves; she twisted her hands together. To anybody walking by she looked like someone about to receive a serious telling off. Tabitha and Lauren stood next to her, but Daisy hadn't turned up. No matter what the ghost and spirit said to reassure her it didn't make her feel any better; she really didn't want to go into the classroom without a living friend with her. What if Mr. Gibb got angry and started shouting at her? What if he thought she was trying to play a trick on him and her parents were called in? What if...?

"Sorry, sorry!" Daisy panted as she came running up behind her. "Miss Fagan always gets excited when it comes to History – I thought she was never going to finish. Are you okay? No, you're not are you? Stupid question, sorry."

"I will be when this is over," Megan replied, her voice shaking with nerves.

"You look like you're going to throw up. Just take a moment to breathe."

"If I stand here for much longer I'm going to chicken out," Megan knocked on the door.

"Come in," Mr. Gibb called.

Tom Gibb was sitting at his desk marking a large pile of books. He looked up and smiled kindly. He knew Daisy although he'd never taught her. He'd been told by those who had that she was bright and pleasant enough, though there was something about her. 'It isn't her face' Peggy Fagan had said, 'you get used to that!' The way Peggy had a pulled a face and shuddered had really annoyed him. He often wondered why Peggy had become a schoolteacher because she didn't seem to enjoy it.

He had seen the other girl in the playground whilst on duty. She was a tall, skinny thing, who reminded him a bit of a scarecrow. Clare Barnet had said she was a nice girl but struggled with Maths. She was however an absolutely fantastic artist. The girl was looking at him as though he was about to shout at her; she was pale with fear. He hated feeling that he had such an effect on a child.

"Hello ladies," he said pleasantly hoping he would put the girl at ease. "How can I help you?"

He couldn't see his dead wife leaning close to him and

shaking her head sadly. "He's lost so much weight," she muttered.

Megan opened her mouth and nerves tightened her throat. It felt impossible to speak so she closed her mouth quickly.

"It's okay," Tabitha said soothingly, "Tell him why you're here and that you understand he'll find it hard to believe. That's the gentle way to do it."

Daisy took hold of Megan's hand, her fingers wrapping around it like a glove, warm and comforting.

"Mr. Gibb, I know that this sounds really, really crazy but I can see ghosts." Megan said slowly and carefully, "and I've seen your wife. She's here, and she would like to talk to you."

Mr Gibb didn't shout; he sat unblinking looking from one girl to the other before carefully putting his pen down. He rubbed his top lip with his index finger.

"Oh dear," Lauren said softly, "he's cross."

Tabitha blinked. "That's cross?"

"Listen girls," Mr Gibb said in a low voice, "my wife didn't die in a very nice way. I'm sure you've heard about it. What you're saying isn't funny, it's very hurtful."

"It's not a joke, Mr Gibb," Megan said, her voice trembling.

"Well, what is it all about then?" Mr Gibb asked. "Are you trying to scare me? Upset me? What? What made you think of something like this?"

Megan thought that he didn't sound angry but that he sounded kind of disappointed.

"Sometimes I wished he would have shouted or thrown things," Lauren said. "When he spoke like this – God, it made me feel so guilty."

Tabitha lit a cigarette and she looked at Megan. "Tell him about the photograph."

Megan nodded. Lauren had told her the story whilst they had been waiting for Daisy. She swallowed down hard and garbled out the memory. "The very first photograph that was taken of you and Lauren, you weren't even together." Mr Gibb continued to glare at her but Megan knew it was too late to go any way but forwards. "It was on your first day of university and your friend, David, took the photograph outside the university's main entrance. Lauren was coming through the door at that very moment. You met each other a few months later at a party, and when you started dating David found the photograph and gave it to you. You took it as a sign that it was all meant to be. You kept it in a silver photo frame on the mantelpiece – you still have it in your bedside drawer." Megan took a deep breath wondering how he was going to react. He was totally still and she thought that she could actually see his heart tearing. She knew it was painful but he had to believe her. "You found her wedding ring by the photo when you came home for lunch and you were so angry that you threw the photo across the room. The glass broke and when you bent down to pick it up, you cut your thumb really badly, that's why you've got a scar there. You were running...

"Stop! Please stop!" Mr Gibbs voice was thick with grief.

Daisy gave Megan's hand a gentle squeeze and whispered, "It's okay, he believes you."

Lauren walked through the desk and crouched down so that she was face to face with her husband.

"I wish I could take back what I said," she whispered. Tears ran down her cheeks. "It was just a party – a stupid party. It didn't matter – not really. You love the kids so much and that's one of the many reasons I love you."

Mr Gibbs had screwed his face into his hand hoping to hide his tears. For one fleeting moment, Megan thought that maybe he could hear his wife's voice.

"Please tell him about the ring. Tell him that it was a misunderstanding; a terrible twist of fate."

"Mr. Gibb, your wife, Lauren, wasn't leaving you. Her

ring was loose – she didn't want to lose it. It was too special.

"How do you know all this?" he asked incredulously.

"She came to see me."

"Is she here now?"

Megan nodded.

"Can she hear me?"

Megan nodded again. "If you speak, she can hear you, although you won't be able to hear her."

A long silence fell between them. Mr Gibb was clearly embarrassed and very overwhelmed. "Will she stay for a while once you've gone?"

Megan looked at Lauren and saw her nodding her head. "Yes, she'll stay for a while but then she has to go and she won't be coming back. She thinks that you need to move on."

Mr Gibbs pressed his lips together and shuddered with the weight of his breath.

"There's something that she wants you to hear before we go. Is that alright?"

Mr Gibbs mouthed, "Yes."

"Megan, I want you to repeat what I say." Lauren said.

"Okay." It felt strange to be speaking so personally to a stranger.

"The way you care for the kids, the way your face lit up when you told me how one of them finally understood how to solve a problem, and the stories you told me about your days made me love you even more. I only said what I did was because I was having a bad week, and I didn't want to be alone in my misery." She shook her head, "God, what did you see in me? I'm bad tempered, self-absorbed..."

"No, you were never any of those things," he said croakily.

"Tell him," Lauren said softly, "tell him I see how the children miss him; they miss the teacher he used to be. Tell him it's time to let go of regrets and for us to say goodbye."

When Megan had had finished Lauren leaned in and kissed Mr. Gibb's cheek. Instinctively he placed his hand where her ghostly lips had touched.

"We're going to go now. Lauren will be with you for about five minutes." Megan told him.

"Thank you, girls," he said shakily.

"Are you going to be okay, Mr Gibb?" Megan asked.

Mr. Gibb nodded and cleared his throat. "Yes, I think I'm going to be just fine," he said, and he gave a small smile. "Thank you."

Megan, Daisy and Tabitha waited outside of the classroom for Lauren. Tabitha needed to show her the way now that things here were finished. Megan had to admit that she was curious to know what would happen to Lauren.

When Lauren arrived, she was crying but she was also happy. Tabitha took her by the hand and pulled her in for a hug. A shower of golden stars spun around their embracing forms and then there was just Tabitha.

"She's passed on," Tabitha said by way of explanation.

Daisy walked with Megan to the school gates. The events of that afternoon span round in Megan's mind. It all seemed like it had been a dream, a very odd dream.

"Are you okay?" Daisy asked her gently. Megan shrugged. She had done so much talking that it felt as though she had used up all her words. Daisy pulled out a piece of paper from her pocket. "This is my phone number – if you need to talk about anything just give me a call, okay?"

Megan took the piece of paper and smiled. "Thank you."

Cheryl was waiting for her and not looking too pleased about having been made to wait in a car with a grumpy toddler. Megan got in apologising and waved to Daisy as they pulled away.

"Got everything sorted with your homework?" she

asked.

For a moment Megan wondered what her Mum was talking about, and then she remembered the lie she had asked Scott to tell when he saw her. It didn't feel easy.

"Yes thanks," she said. "I think I understand everything now."

Cheryl frowned. She sensed something different about her daughter but she wasn't exactly sure what it was.

"Are you alright?" she asked.

Megan looked at her and weighed up the possibility of telling her and then dismissed it. How could she tell her Mum that since coming to Threshold she had found out Witches and magic were real, and not just in fairy-tales? And even crazier, how could she tell her mum that she'd just learned that she had been born with a special gift? One that she still wasn't convinced wasn't a curse.

In the end she sighed and said, "I'm fine. It's just been a really busy day."

11. JACK

Jack Rowan walked home from his Psychometry lesson eating chips (with probably far too much vinegar and definitely more salt than was needed) from a bag. Jack liked his chips just like this – and after all it was his birthday. He knew from bitter experience that the children at school would tease him about his birthday being on Halloween. His dad always told him it was because they were jealous as it made him extra special. Of course no one at school knew just how special he was. Nobody was allowed to know because, as Dad reminded him (often), look how Mum had used him because of his gifts.

Jack pretended to burn his mouth on a chip to make up an excuse for the tears in his eyes. He was still at that stage where he could almost fully believe his own lies. Mum could be fun; she would sing to him, dance him around until he was dizzy, taught him how to garden and a whole load of other things that his dad never really valued. She had been a good mum – it was only when she drank too much that she became nasty; losing her temper easily, shouting, and hitting out at anything she loved. She had been getting better (or so Jack had told himself) but then she had fallen in with what Dad called a bad crowd down at the pub. It was the bad crowd that had tricked her into thinking that taking tablets would be just as much fun as drinking – they were after all the same tablets the doctors gave you to make you feel better. The only thing was that tablets cost money, even more than drink. Mum wasn't a very educated lady but she was resourceful. She soon understood that her son had a gift and a talent that could be turned into a very lucrative little business. She would take Jack out with the bad crowd and they would give him objects to touch – things like clothes and keys, stuff like that. Jack's job was to use his gift to tell them if he could find out anything really bad about the person who owned it. The more information he gave them, the more love and affection his mother showed him. Sometimes she would even give him a couple of quid as a treat. Jack didn't' really understand that they were using him so they could blackmail the 'bad people'.

The night Dad found out what was going on, Mum had come into his room with a paperweight. It had been made of glass and had little bubbles in it. He wanted to make her happy. It had been over a week since she had last hugged him and told him that she loved him. As soon as he touched it everything inside him went mad. It was as if his body were trying to feel every sensation known. His emotions fought each other, all wanting to be felt first. Somewhere in a place that seemed very far away, he could hear his Mum screaming.

When he woke up it was morning, he was tucked up in bed. At first he thought it had been a nightmare until he saw Dad sitting in a chair next to him. He looked very tired and upset. Although after school every Friday Mrs Cooper (a seemingly quaint old lady from the village) had been teaching him how to use his ability, it seemed that everyone had underestimated the strength of his abilities. Mum hadn't checked the history of the object she'd asked him to touch. The violence of the reaction was because of the violence connected to it. Dad told Jack's mother to go: he didn't want her anywhere near Jack again.

Dad was waiting, as was his habit, at the corner of the road. He waited there every day in order to keep Jack company on the last leg of his walk home. Jack hadn't the heart to say that he was a big boy now and that he didn't need supervising.

"Alright Jack?" Dad had asked. "You're very quiet."

"I'm enjoying my chips," Jack said looking up at him and smiling. "They're great. Want one?"

Jack's dad shook his head. He knew his son was lying. He ruffled Jack's hair and Jack made a show of being bothered by it.

"How about when we get home I read you that book you got from your girlfriend?" his dad asked.

"Dad! Give over! Carol is my best friend." Jack sighed. "She's *not* my girlfriend... That would be just too weird, trust me."

His dad laughed but it was cut short. He stopped and stared down the path in front of them.

Jack looked and saw someone who looked like his Mum standing in the path. She looked older – too thin, like she hadn't eaten for ages. Her hair was limp and dull and her skin was a horrible grey colour.

"Jackie!" She approached with a wide smile on her face. "Happy birthday sweetheart!"

"What do you want, Jenny?" His Dad demanded. He'd instinctively stood in front of Jack, protecting him.

"I've come to show my son that I'm better," his mum said coolly. "I thought that would be the best birthday present I could give him."

Jack glanced round at his Dad. Mum didn't look like

she was better – there was something not right about her; it was like looking at a picture that hung slightly crooked.

"You don't look better," his dad replied. "Far from it. What do really want?"

"I want my son," his mum said, holding out her hands towards Jack. "Come on sweetheart, touch Mummy's hand and tell Daddy how much better she is."

"With the history you're carrying around with you, I don't want you even breathing on him. And don't talk to him like that; he's not a baby."

She pouted in return, not liking that she wasn't getting her own way. His dad took a step forward indicating that he meant business. "It's getting dark and it's time we we're going home. If I see you anywhere near our house, Jenny, then I'll call the police."

"A child's place is always with their Mother," his mum said looking at Jack.

"Not when the 'mother' uses the child's abilities to fund their drug and alcohol addiction," Dad replied taking Jack gently by the hand. Jack felt like he was literally at the centre of a tug of war rope.

All at once two men came out from the bushes and stood either side of his mum. Jack moved closer to Dad – as he had said, it was getting dark, and the moon had started to rise. It was big and round: a full moon with beams that peeked through the leafless branches.

"What?" Dad frowned looking at the two men. "Do you seriously think you're going to take him by force?"

"No, Rick," his Mum grinned showing a mouth full of sharp teeth, "by tooth and claw."

With that the two men quickly began to change.

"Jack," his dad shouted, "run!"

He threw his chips down and ran – he ran hard, until his heart was thumping in his chest, his lungs were screaming for air, and his throat was burning. He risked a glance back to see if his Dad was running with him. To his horror, his Dad wasn't there.

Jack hadn't heard his Dad fall. Where was he? He heard footsteps running up the path and started to laugh with relief, still not entirely believing the craziness of the situation until he saw what sprang around the corner. All Jack could see was a mixed up image of sharp grinning teeth and slashing claws. The rest of the creature was fur. The stench of iron travelled across the short space between them. Blood. His fathers? Jack knew he couldn't outrun the thing, but he could climb. Surely it would be too heavy to follow after him? Jack scrambled up the trunk of the nearest tree and leapt for the branch. He got it and he felt a fleeting sense of triumph. He swung his legs up with the intention of wrapping himself safely around the branch only to have a pair of strong jaws clamp around his ankle, biting hard. Jack felt hot searing pain; something had broken. Then the pain receded, overtaken by a sensory assault – the contact between the beast and Jack caused a rapid psychometric connection. Jack could feel everything this terrible creature had ever done. It was too much; his hands couldn't hold onto the branch, and he fell.

Jack woke soaked with sweat from his nightmare. Every single muscle shook. He ached right down to his bones. Wrapping his arms around himself, he tried to settle his breathing. It was over he reminded himself, the pack had gone: he had been promised that they were gone. It was over. He was safe. Another shudder went through him and he gritted his teeth, telling himself firmly that he was now forty-one years old, not eight. Despite the fact that he hadn't heard from the pack for years (they'd sold him out to 'The Place' when he had refused to join them; a fate worse than death.) Jack always felt their presence at his back.

"Jack?" Una's soft voice came from the doorway. "Are you alright? I heard a noise."

Jack sat up in his chair. He hadn't meant to fall asleep; he'd only meant to sit down for a few seconds until his leg stopped hurting. Even though years had passed since the attack, his leg refused to fully heal. Una looked at him with concern. The expression reminded him of Una's son, Allen. Allen had been part of the investigation team that brought down 'The Place'. The investigation started because a newly employed scientist discovered exactly was going on there: evil.

It had been Allen who had forced open the door of the laboratory and freed him. It had been Allen, his saviour, who had patiently worked with him, won his trust and fixed him up as best he ever could be. When the investigation was over, Allen arranged for Jack to live with Una; a place where he would be safe and protected. Jack could never thank Allen enough for the gift of Una; she was the mother his own had failed to be.

"Jack?" Una walked over to him.

"Sorry, I'm fine," he said, hating the way his voice shook. "Do you need any help with Patrick?"

"He's sleeping." Una sat down on the arm of his chair. "Which was what you were doing, until you had a nightmare." She took Jack's hand. "When have you ever been able to fool me, Jack Rowan?"

"I'm sorry," Jack said quietly. "Did I wake you? Of course I woke you." He looked at the kitchen door. "Have I woken Daisy?"

"No," Una replied. She's exhausted poor little mite."

"That's probably my fault." Jack sighed and shifted in his seat. "I convinced her to befriend Megan, she already does so much, I didn't think…"

"Ssh! She's got a friend her own age and she's going to a sleepover tomorrow." Una smiled, deciding it probably not a good idea to tell him that she had invested two hours to convince Daisy to go. "She's loving it. It's good for her to try normal for a change. Anyways, I think she would have picked up Megan's need even without your suggestion." Una stood and headed towards the kettle. "But she's not the only one who does too much; you've absorbed a lot of histories today, haven't you? Shouldn't you let them go?"

"I can't." Jack ran his hand tight across his eyes. "I need to make sure that I've not missed anything important."

There was a time when Una would be able to hold him and use her warm healing energy to dissolve the darkness of the histories he absorbed. Her gift would sooth his muscles and let him sleep. Sometimes he'd sleep for a week, only waking for water. But she'd lost her gift:

thrown it away. Now all she could do was make herbal remedies that relieved her loved ones of their problems for a short while but soon faded. Una wished she could undo the past; go back to the time she had so carelessly misused her gift for wrong. But she couldn't. Her punishment was a life-sentence.

12. SCOTT'S CHOICE

Scott kicked the fallen leaves all the way to school. He was sad. He hurt inside. He should have been used to the continual disappointments his father gifted by now. Even though his dad had promised, really promised with a shake of the hand and everything, his Dad had failed to pick him up from school last night. Although he loved his Granddad very much, Scott's heart had still sunk when he saw his Granddad's battered old car waiting for him outside the school gate. Dad had phoned Mum and told her that he was in a very important meeting that he just couldn't leave. He was sure that Scott would understand. Granddad had taken him out for burger and chips and then they had gone to the cinema. His granddad was a kind man so Scott had really tried to enjoy himself but it wasn't the same as it would have been with his dad.

Tim and April (friends since playgroup days) came up along side him. They had got to know when there had been another dad-let-down-incident and they tried their best to cheer him up – not today though, today they were on another mission. They looked serious. Scott sighed, he really didn't want 'serious' before school; he had enough of that already.

"Scott we want to talk to you about Megan," Tim said.

Scott frowned. He hadn't expected that. "What about her?"

"She's weird," April said. "Yesterday, Pippa heard her talking to herself in the library."

Scott knew she was probably talking to Tabitha thinking she was alone, but he wasn't going to tell his friends that; some people thought that talking to ghosts and spirits was creepy.

"She was probably thinking out aloud." Scott shrugged. "We all do that."

April shook her head. "No, Pippa said this was a proper conversation and there was nobody else there."

"So, she's different! What's the problem?" Scott asked. "She's nice, I thought you liked her."

"She is nice," Tim said, "but to be honest, we're only being friendly with her because you asked us to. Besides, she's best friend with Daisy and that just isn't going to work for us – we've got our reputation to think about. "

"What reputation?" Scott asked, stifling a laugh. "You don't have a reputation."

"Exactly," April said. "We're normal."

Tim, still not sure that Scott had got the message hammered the point home. "And if you hang round with them, people are going to start to think you're like them – weird."

"And not in a cool way," April added. "Being interested in the paranormal, well that's cool. We like you because of it, but ..." She glanced at Tim looking for help.

"What we're trying to say is that we can't be seen with you if you're going to be friends with Megan and Daisy." Tim said.

If Scott hadn't been so genuinely shocked by his friends' outrageous behaviour then he might have found some kind of heroic response. Instead he carried on walking, slightly slack-jaw and finding it hard to keep his breathing regular.

"And why would you want to be friends with Daisy anyway?" April asked. "She covers herself with animal-blood and dances naked in the woods!"

"I definitely do not do that!" came a familiar voice from behind them. "I catch cold really easily so nudity is out, and I'm a vegetarian, which throws the animal blood thing right out of the window."

April and Tim spun round to face a very hard and angry Daisy.

April's whole body language changed. She leaned in close to Scott and whispered, "Scott you've got to tell her that we're sorry," April said. "Last time someone upset Daisy, they got scabies!"

"Oh for goodness sake, get a grip! That was nothing to do with her," Scott said crossly. "Why don't you just grown up and say sorry yourself?" He adjusted his bag on his shoulder and strode off calling behind him, "Coming Daisy?"

"Did you have a good time with your Dad?" Daisy asked not looking at him.

"He didn't come," Scott said flatly. "He had a really important meeting and he couldn't get away; he'll make it up to me when I go and visit him next weekend. He promised me that we'll go fishing."

"That'll be nice." Daisy held out her half-eaten orange. "Want some?"

"No thanks."

They walked a way in silence, both of them lost in worry about the other. Eventually when the silence became too obvious, Scott plucked up enough courage to ask, "Daisy are you okay? I mean about what Tim and April said – did it bother you?"

"I should be used to it by now, shouldn't I?" Daisy popped a piece of orange into her mouth but continued talking. She didn't need to worry about her manners around Scott. "When Mum and Dad had their whole 'empowerment' moment and announced to the entire village that we were Witches, we had our windows broken and things written on the garden wall that I didn't understand, but they upset Mum. One night, I woke up and found someone had built a bonfire on our front lawn. They'd topped it with a shop mannequin dressed in a witch's Halloween costume. I guess they thought that was witty – either that or they were trying to conduct their own type of magic."

"Why didn't your Mum and Dad move?" Scott asked. "Threshold isn't that far from your village and you'd have been much more welcome here." He smiled " There are a lot of us weird folk here," he joked.

"They said that they weren't going to run away; they were on a mission to 'educate' everybody about what really exists in this world. They said it would mean that no one would have to hide anymore – or be ashamed." Daisy's voice betrayed the fact that part of her still felt ashamed of what she was, and Scott knew exactly how that felt. In that moment he wondered how Daisy might react if he were to take her hand in his and let her know that she really wasn't alone: that someone in this world liked her for being just exactly who she was.

Daisy sighed, "They said it would pass, that once people saw that, apart from the magic, we were just like them with jobs, friends and family, they wouldn't be afraid of us anymore. They always believed the best in people." She stopped walking and turned to Scott, reading his expression. "Threshold isn't that much different from my village. They still attack with their words. Whoever said sticks and stones may break my bones, but names shall never hurt me was wrong. They hurt.

Scott nodded in sympathy. "Yeah, tell me about that one. Granddad calls it death by a thousand cuts."

"I get that. You know this wasn't the first school my Nan chose, she wanted me to go to Winterbournes; it's closer to my home, but some parents heard I was coming and they gave the Head a petition with over a thousand signatures from people who didn't want me to go there. It shouldn't bother me but it does."

"They," he nodded behind them to indicate Tim and

April, "told me that they don't want to be seen with Megan anymore. Someone overheard her having a conversation with Tabitha so they think she's weird. They think that if they let her near them it'll ruin their reputation."

"Their world is going to be a very dull place if they don't open their minds to interesting things and people," Daisy said bitterly. "She's going to be upset, you know that don't you? Of course being friends with me probably didn't do her any favours."

"I've known those two a long time and now they want me to choose."

Daisy was about to say something, but she stopped. Megan was approaching and she looked worried.

"Looks serious – what are you talking about?" she asked.

Scott wasn't sure what to say. He fidgeted on the spot and opened his mouth several times before shrugging.

Daisy stepped in to the rescue. "April and Tim think me and Scott shouldn't be friends because I'm bad for his reputation. According to them I dance naked, covered in animal's blood, on moonlit nights."

"But you're a vegetarian," Megan frowned.

"Exactly!" Daisy nodded, she looked across the playground and saw Tim and April looking at her nervously. "What precisely do they think I'm going to do to them?"

Scott looked at Daisy, he knew she was lying to protect Megan, but wouldn't she find out? And then she wouldn't be angry with her for lying? Megan was still frowning.

"I'll go and talk to them," she said.

"No, it's okay," Daisy said. "I need to go and clear this up with them. I'll be back in a minute."

Tim and April looked horrified as Daisy approached them.

"I'm not going to do anything nasty, I promise," Daisy said.

"We're really sorry that we upset you," Tim said. "We just care about Scott and we don't want people to start thinking... "

"Stop lying to me," Daisy said.

"I'm not lying," Tim protested. "If you really cared for him you'd..." Tim's words faded out because Daisy's green eyes were glowing softly. April watched on. She wanted to run but her feet were firmly stuck to the ground.

Daisy smiled triumphantly. "Don't worry, it won't be forever; just long enough for you to listen to me." She stepped in close and lowered her voice, aware that Scott and Megan were watching on closely. "You're only friends with Scott because his Mum is your Dad's boss; he told you to be nice to him." She turned her attention to April. "And you, you're only nice to him because he basically does all of your homework. He thinks you two losers really like him so sort this out by going and telling him that he's entitled to be friends with whomever he pleases. You have no idea how much you hurt him asking him to choose. And if Megan ever found out what you said, she'd hurt too – I don't like my friends hurting.

As Daisy walked away April found to her relief that she could at last move her feet.

"What are we going to do?" she whispered.

"Exactly what she told us to do," Tim said with a tongue that felt strangely tingly. "And we don't tell anyone what just happened, right?"

April nodded.

13. PSYCHS, MAGICKS, PARANATURALS & BLANDS

Theo had completely forgotten that Megan was having a sleepover until he tripped over three pair of shoes in the hallway. Dad radar immediately caused him to notice that one of those pairs belonged to a boy. He didn't remember Megan saying that a boy was coming to her sleepover. He wasn't sure that he was too happy about that; it wasn't like she was still at primary school anymore.

He walked into the living room, placed his briefcase next to the chair by the fireplace (known as Dad's chair seeing as he had laid claim to it the day they'd moved in). Tyler came running up to him and he ruffled the little tykes hair. He swung by Cheryl, bent down and kissed her on the cheek, which she offered coldly. Rejected, he headed towards the warmth of the fire when he noticed a collection of crystals lined up on the mantelpiece.

"What on earth are they?" he asked.

"Daisy brought them with her. They're to help him with Tyler's asthma." Cheryl walked over and started pointing them out, "Erm, I think that's morganite. Amber. Beryl, and Azurite. I can't remember what the other four are. I'll have to ask her later."

"And how are crystals supposed to help with asthma?" Theo asked raising his eyebrows.

Cheryl sighed. "You know, some people have found alternative medicine actually works."

"You can't call this mumbo jumbo medicine," Theo retorted. "Honestly, Cheryl... our daughter's new friend is a hippy? Didn't you say her Granddad has dementia? Did her grandmother give you the impression that they believe that crystals and herbs are enough to cure him?"

"Daisy told me the crystals wouldn't heal Tyler but that they'd help boost the medicine he's taking." Cheryl folded her arms. "I thought it was a very nice gesture, and no she's not a hippy! I can't exactly put my finger one what she is but it doesn't matter; she's Megan's friend and she makes her smile – really smile, something I haven't seen Megan do in quite a while so could you put your opinions on hold for one evening?"

Theo huffed. "Am I allowed to express my opinion about how my daughter is having a boy at her sleepover?" Theo asked.

"If you'd bothered to listen to your daughter the other

day then you'll know Scott is just staying for tea. She didn't want him to feel left out. And even if he were staying the night, it wouldn't be a problem. Why don't you go and say hello before you start making opinions on *our* daughter's friends."

Theo noticed how the word 'our' was stressed but the look that surfaced in Cheryl's eyes meant he decided not to make any more comments. Instead he left to go and introduce himself.

He'd not realised before how cold the stairs leading up to Megan's room were. Mind he rarely went up there. 'Maybe we should get a radiator put somewhere' he thought. He was lost in these practical thoughts when the sound of a very loud thump made Theo jump. For one moment he thought that something had fallen from the ceiling. He raced into Megan's room and found her sat crossed legged next to a somewhat chunky boy (who really aught to be going on a preventative diet) and a girl with some of the worst burn scars he'd come across. The girl sat very straight backed on Megan's desk chair.

"What was that bang?" Theo asked. He had a feeling it had something to do with the chair otherwise why would it be in the middle of the room like it was.

"Sorry about that. I was showing Megan and Scott a

dance move I saw on television," the girl said, standing up and holding out her hand. "Hello, I'm Daisy."

Theo took hold of the girl's hand and shook it. His doctor-brain refused to disengage and he found himself still awkwardly holding her hand after completing a full analysis of her face. He was left wondering how on Earth she'd managed to survive the cause of such scars. He vaguely remembered Cheryl telling him about it that day she'd met Daisy at the library but he had though she had been exaggerating.

"Hi, I'm Scott." The boy didn't get up but gave a small wave.

"I'm Theo, Megan's Dad. Are you all warm enough in here?"

All three of them nodded.

"Right, okay, well, I'll leave you to your dancing then."

Megan waited until she was sure Dad was gone before she looked at Tabitha. "Thanks for the warning."

Tabitha smiled. "Not a problem." Part of her wished she hadn't called out a warning to Megan. After what the esteemed Dr. Theo had been saying about the crystals and Daisy, she would have felt very satisfied seeing his expression at seeing a chair circling the bedroom.

"Yes, thanks Tabitha," Daisy said picking up the chair and putting it back by the desk.

"That was really cool." Scott beamed. "What else can you do?"

"I think I'd better not do anymore demonstrations," Daisy said. "I'm not a good liar."

"Yes, we noticed that. Dance moves?" Megan asked with a smile.

"It's the only thing I could think of."

The trio burst out in a fit of giggles. It felt good to be friends.

"Right, love you and leave you, I'm off to see Lady Agatha," Tabitha declared. "She haunts the Royal Oak, she doesn't want to cross over because she has far too much fun where she is."

"Tabitha's going to visit one of her friends," Megan translated. "She won't be here to listen out for us."

"Have fun," Daisy said pulling out a large book from her bag. " I think it'll be okay to give you this now. It doesn't look interesting enough for adults to have a nosey at it but you might want to think about a good hiding place anyhow."

The book looked like one of those very old (and hardly ever used) encyclopaedias. Daisy placed it carefully in front of Megan before sitting down cross-legged opposite her.

"Uncle Jack got this from Mrs Cooper. She's a very powerful Psych," Daisy informed them. "It's a kind of help book for people who are like you and whose parents don't have any psychic ability. It might answer some questions that Tabitha and me can't answer. I had a look and it's not like a boring textbook; it's interesting and actually has some funny bits in it which surprised me."

"What's a Psych?" Scott asked.

"People who have psychic abilities and what some would call a supernatural ability. I thought your Granddad would have told you that."

"He can only tell me what he knows," Scott said. "He told me everything that's in fairy-tales, myths, legends, nightmares, that they're real, but you guys!" Scott laughed until he had tears in his eyes but this time the others were silent which ended up being funny in itself, and before long all three of them were gasping for breath and fending off hiccups.

Daisy stopped laughing, suddenly attacked by a profound feeling of sadness. This right here – this this friendship and acceptance was something her parents had fought so hard for; sacrificing everything including their lives. Maybe if they had started slower, with one good friend at a time then they would still be alive because more people would have protected them.

She cleared her throat and pulled herself together. She didn't want to bring everybody down with her mood change.

"Time for some proper education, Scotty Boy. Things and people in this world can be separated into four main groups. There are Psychs, that's people like Megan, and Telekinetics, Empaths, Clairvoyants." She paused and looked at the fingers she'd been using to tick them off. "Actually there are way more than four – it's a pretty long list actually." She let her hands fall realising that they weren't much use and continued. "Then there are Magicks, that's magic with a k on the end, that's what I am, and any beings or creatures you'll find in fairy stories unicorns, fairies, trolls; then there are Paranaturals, which are beings who are supernatural and paranormal; Shape-shifters, Chupacabras, ghosts, spirits. Then there are animals and people like... like Scott."

"And what are they called?" Megan asked.

Daisy looked uncomfortable. "I don't really like the word."

"Aww, come on, I want to know what I'm called,"

Scott said.

"You're a... a Bland," Daisy replied softly. Megan and Scott looked at her blankly. "Bland means dull, routine, commonplace, boring. You can't get any more ordinary than being bland." She shook her head before garbling, "Which you're not Scott, just because you can't see ghosts or spirits, or do magic, I mean Marie Curie, Alexander Fleming, Mother Teresa... they couldn't and look what they could do."

"It's just a word," Scott shrugged. "I'm not going to get upset about it."

Daisy wondered if he would be if he knew that Psyches, Paranaturals and Magicks used the word as an insult. If someone couldn't use their abilities very well, or they were weak then they would be accused of being a Bland.

14. THE VISIT

Tabitha wasn't going to see Lady Agatha. Although she did exist and she did find her antics very amusing, she really wasn't in the mood for them, not today. Spirits can go anywhere they want, just by thinking it, and Tabitha's thoughts didn't take her to The Royal Oak. It took her to a modest semi-detached house, near the center of a small seaside town.

She looked around the bedroom she found herself admiring the artwork on the walls, and resisting the urge to pick up the small teddy bear sitting on the writing table, next to a photograph. She didn't want to scare the owner of the room by finding a toy floating in mid- air.

She didn't have to wait long; she heard the front door shut.

"Paige," a man's voice called, "is that you?"

"Yeah," a girl's voice called back. "I'm just going upstairs, I'll be down in a sec."

The bedroom door opened and a seventeen-year-old girl walked in carrying shopping bags, which she put on her bed. She was short and with what Tabitha considered, curves in all the right places. She had long, black, straight hair and dark eyes that looked out from a baby doll face.

With a smile Paige removed her jacket and quickly took off her top so she was standing in her bra. Before she turned her back to the mirror on the wall, she removed the piece of gauze that had been placed on her shoulder and admired the newly done tattoo of a pentagram entwined with forget-me-nots. .

Tabitha sighed. "Oh Paige, why couldn't you have waited until next year? If your uncle sees that…"

"Would you have approved of it next year?" a voice said behind her.

"Probably not." She shrugged.

Paige's phone rang and she quickly ran to her handbag. On answering it she grinned from ear to ear.

"You know that she got it to honor your memory," the voice said.

"I still don't approve." Tabitha responded quietly. "But it's her body."

A gentle hand was placed onto her shoulder. "Don't do this to yourself Tabitha, it only upsets you."

"It's my birthday, Arthur," Tabitha said, finally turning round and looking at the voice's owner. "Can't I do what I want on my birthday?"

Arthur was a small man whose long hair was tied into a ponytail. His bright blue eyes looked at her sadly.

"Birthdays should be a happy time."

"I am happy. I'm happy that I'm seeing her. Why isn't that okay?"

"Because it's the past, and you've got someone else to look after remember?"

Tabitha watched Paige take her new clothes out of the bags, and hang them up in the wardrobe.

"I think they made a mistake about me," she said. "I'm honestly not cut out to be a child's spirit guide; I'm short tempered, Megan needs someone who has a heck of a lot more patience, and probably a much better role model, and someone who has a clear idea of what is going on. Why the Hell do we not shadow someone experienced before we're sent out on our own is beyond me."

Arthur smiled. "They don't make mistakes."

"Yeah, well there's a first time for everything." Tabitha sighed.

"They made their choice," Arthur said. "Your concern for the child shows that you are more cut out then you think."

Paige took a small candle over to the photograph on the table and placed it down gently.

"Uncle Ken said you loved the smell of cinnamon," she said, taking a box of matches from the drawer.

Tabitha moved closer and watched Paige light it. The girl kissed the tips of her fingers and placed it gently onto the photograph.

"Happy birthday," she whispered.

Tabitha moved closer wishing that she could plant a kiss on the back of Paige's head, but it wouldn't make any difference, she would just think that it was her imagination. She smiled sadly.

"Thank you sweetheart, happy birthday to you too."

15. FULL MOON

Megan woke to find her bedroom full of moonlight. She thought the terrible howl that had woken her had been part of the strange dream that she had been having but then she noticed Daisy standing by the window looking out across the woods.

"What's wrong?" Megan whispered.

"I need to go outside for a little while," Daisy said softly. "I won't be long."

"I'll come with you," Megan replied sitting up.

"No, I need to go alone." Daisy picked up her bag and retrieved two small pouches. "Stay here!" she instructed firmly.

With that she crept out of the room quickly. Megan chewed the bottom of her lip thoughtfully, 'What could Daisy possible be doing this time of the night?' The house was quiet, as if it holding its breath, too afraid to make a sound. Megan began to feel uncomfortable; she certainly didn't want to be alone. As quietly as she could, she got out of bed and followed in Daisy's wake.

However Daisy was nowhere to be seen. Megan sighed heavily, weighing up the probability that she had headed out towards the woods.

It was a cold frosty night and Megan was glad she had put on her thick dressing gown and slippers. She wrapped her arms around herself as she walked past the flowerbeds. There was still no sign of Daisy. Reluctantly, she headed through the creaky green gate and headed towards the treeline. A cold wind blew causing her to shiver. The wind not only brought an icy chill but it also carried the sound of sobbing. It was soft and quiet and Megan really had to strain her ears to hear it. Megan didn't like the idea of someone crying out here, alone. However, she needed to find Daisy. Something was seriously wrong.

The woods were much darker than the garden, and it was quiet – very, very quiet. There wasn't a single night creature scuttling, or an owl hooting. Nothing. Just heavy silence. Megan held her breath and listened. It was then she heard a low whine and Daisy's gentle voice. Megan couldn't make out what she was saying but the tone was soft and soothing. She walked towards it, and then wished she had listened to her friend.

Daisy gently stroked the wolf's head, running her fingers through his thick sandy fur. The shock of seeing her friend crouched next to a huge wolf in the middle of the English countryside was enough of a shock to stop her from noticing something very odd about the creature. The creature, sensing the presence of a stranger and possible threat, turned its head towards Daisy and fixed her with eyes that she could only describe as being human.

"No!" she gasped. "That can't be true. I'm dreaming."

The creature let out a low moan and Daisy comforted it. "Yes, Megan. It's true. This is what you think it is."

Megan stepped back wondering if she had truly lost her mind. She studied the creature in front of her. Now that she knew, she could see that he was barely wolf shaped at all. The werewolf lay on the floor like a man who walked upright. He was covered in thick wolf fur and where hands should have been, there were wolf feet with thick animal-like claws protruding from them.

To Daisy, he was the most fascinating creature she'd ever seen, even if the fur on his back was thin where he had been burnt and the skin was horribly scarred. Her eyes travelled down to the jagged mouth of the gin trap. He'd been biting into his already damaged ankle when she had found him. Daisy had removed it easily with a spell, and would have loved to have melted the horrible contraption into a satisfying lump of metal but that would have used too much energy; she needed that to heal the ankle the best she could. There wasn't anything she could do with the broken bone, she wasn't strong enough for that, but she could heal the skin.

"Bloody hell, Megan." Daisy stood up. "Which part of 'I need to do this alone, stay here' didn't you understand? You've broken the spell."

The werewolf crawled over to Megan who could feel her heart thumping in her chest. At first she though she couldn't move because she was so afraid, but the more she tried to move the more the air around her grew colder and tighter. She knew it must be a spell. Daisy stood watching her. Megan felt a lump form in her throat. She had thought Daisy was her friend but she was going to stand by and let this monster tear her apart. Tears ran down her cheeks. She wanted her Mum and Dad: she didn't want to die. Megan closed her eyes not wanting to face what was coming to her. She waited, and waited, and then ever so gently a rough warm tongue licked her tears away. 'Oh, my God, he's tasting me!' she thought. The werewolf blew on hair, and then she heard him dragging himself away.

Megan slowly opened her eyes, genuinely surprised to

find that she was still alive. The werewolf was croached next to Daisy who was stroking him behind the ears. He looked at her with his one eye a deep warm brown, and the other, an icy blue. Megan knew that she'd seen those eyes before.

"I'm going to let you go now," Daisy said. "I needed you to see that he wasn't going to hurt you before you went screaming back home."

The air warmed around her and the tightness disappeared.

"You could have just told me that your Uncle Jack is a werewolf," she protested. "I wouldn't have run."

"You ran away from your own gift the first time you knew about it," Daisy reminded her. "If you hadn't noticed, there's a hotel with guests in over there. Not many people pay attention when an animal howls, but a child screaming! I've already used a lot of energy to heal his foot the best I can and to put a small protection spell around him. People are dangerous when they're scared."

"You really think someone would have believed me if I'd told them there was a monster in the woods?" Megan asked.

"Don't!" Daisy said sharply. "Don't call him a *monster*. A monster isn't what you are; it's *who* you are.

When I was little I used to forward to full moons and Uncle Jack's transformations."

"How did all this happen?" Megan asked.

"You're either born a werewolf, or you're made into one. Jack's Mum made him into one."

"His mum?"

Daisy nodded. "Uncle Jack's Mum left him with his Dad. She drank too much and took drugs. She joined a gang of criminals, which she soon left for a more powerful gang. You see, Jack's mother was aware of her son's gifts and knew exactly how to sell them out to the highest bidders: who just happened to be a pack of werewolves.

Her price was to be turned into one herself – and how she enjoyed her new role. It was Jack's own mother that attacked him so badly she nearly killed him." Daisy kissed Jack gently on the head and whispered, "Two werewolves, but only one monster." She looked up at Megan and smiled sadly. "Same could be said about the human race, couldn't it? Some people are okay and others can be complete monsters... you can't always tell from the face " Her hand subconsciously touched her scarred cheek.

Megan wanted to reassure her that she didn't look like a monster – not at all. In fact she looked like the best, most loyal and loving friend in the world. Instead she asked,

"How are we going to hide him?"

Daisy held up one of the pouches she had brought with her. "Some people only see what they want to see," she told her. "Others need a little help."

Megan and Daisy crept through the back door of the tower where the Webb family lived, wincing when the key made a horrible squeaking sound.

"What are you two girls doing up?" asked Cheryl. Both girls jumped guiltily. "Look at the state of your feet!"

Megan and Daisy looked down, their feet were pretty muddy, and Daisy's feet were pale with the cold.

"I'm sorry, it's my fault," Daisy said quietly. "I was walking in my sleep. I've done it before but not for a long time. I should have warned you about it."

"Please don't send her home, Mum," Megan pleaded. She still wasn't sure if Daisy was angry with her for calling Jack a monster.

"Not unless Daisy wants to go home," Cheryl said turning to Daisy.

"I'd like to stay please," Daisy replied.

"Okay, I'll go and get a flannel so you can clean your poor feet." Cheryl looked at Megan, "Take your slippers off and go back up to bed, I won't keep Daisy long."

Cheryl insisted on helping Daisy wash her feet, and then tucked both her and Megan into bed. Megan waited until the house was quiet again before she spoke. "Daisy," she whispered, "I'm sorry I called your uncle a monster."

"I'm sorry I told you off about it," Daisy said from the camp bed. "I need to remember that this is all new to you, I've grown up with it... still growing up with it, there's some things even I don't know about."

"Don't you find that scary?" Megan asked.

"A bit," Daisy answered. "Still that's life isn't it? You don't know everything... it's probably not a good idea to tell Scott about what happened tonight."

"How long will it take for your nan to get to him?"

Daisy had done a small spell so her Nan would get to know that Jack needed her.

Daisy smiled in the gloom, "Knowing Nan, she'll already have him home and tucked up in front of the fire with his leg bandaged up – she's amazingly spritely for her age."

"Do you think Scott would have freaked?" Megan rolled over and looked at Daisy she could see her clearly in the moonlight shining through the window.

"No," she shook her head. "He'll be so disappointed that he missed Jack in his wolf form that we'd never hear the end of it." Daisy smiled.

It was such a relief to know her friend wasn't angry with her Megan couldn't help but giggle.

16. AN EPISODE

"I came downstairs for something to drink and there they were," Cheryl said to Theo as she got breakfast ready. "Megan woke up to find Daisy gone and found her sleepwalking in the garden; the poor little thing her feet were blue with cold." When Theo didn't answer she turned to stare at him. He was sat at the kitchen table reading the newspaper, "Are you listening to a word I'm saying?" she said haughtily.

"Maybe she just fancied dancing in the moonlight," Theo replied without looking up. "It's what her kind of people do, isn't it: to be 'one with nature,' or something like that."

"I think if she wanted to go and look at the moon she would have said." Cheryl sighed turning back to her cooking. "She doesn't seem to be the sort to lie."

"I didn't say she was looking at the moon, I said she was dancing under it," Theo said. "She might have been embarrassed that Megan caught her and made up the story about sleep walking." He picked up his coffee and lowered his voice, "There's something really strange about her but I can't put my finger what it is exactly."

"Maybe it's because my smile is slightly lopsided," Daisy's voice came from behind and Theo winced with the social indelicacy.

Cheryl turned to Daisy with a smile of mortification. Megan, with her hands on her hips, glared at her father with a mixture of hurt and anger on her face. Daisy didn't look at all bothered as she turned her attention to Megan. "Why does everyone think I want to dance in the moonlight?" she asked her with a light laugh in her voice.

"I don't know," Megan replied still glaring fixedly at her Dad. "Dad? Why do you think my best friend is strange?"

"Oh, I know the answer to that," Daisy said. "I gave your Mum some crystals to help with Tyler's asthma; he probably thinks it's all mumbo jumbo and isn't worth giving a try."

"Well," Theo inhaled deeply, "as a doctor I've got to have a scientific mind and the idea of crystals being able to help with any aliment is really quite... ludicrous."

"Dad," Megan protested. She looked to her mum for

support but Cheryl just shrugged. "Where is Tyler this morning?" Megan asked giving Daisy a small conspiritorial smile. "He hasn't coughed once."

"You can't just go on one night," Theo said closing his newspaper. "Cheryl told me about your Granddad – does your Nan use alternative medicine to treat him?"

"She uses the medicines the doctor has given her to 'treat' Granddad and we use alternative medicine to help him be more comfortable," Daisy said. "Nan uses aromatherapy and massage, and Uncle Jack plays the violin."

Cheryl placed a large plate of freshly baked croissants in the middle of the table. "Is your uncle a musician, Daisy?" she asked.

"It's more a hobby. He's actually a forensic pathologist. He has a scientific mind too... and an open one!" The tone of Daisy's voice was unusually sharp.

"Come and have some breakfast girls," Cheryl said giving Theo the 'don't-say-another-word' look.

Cheryl had just started with the pancakes when there was a knock at the kitchen door. Theo frowned, wondering who would come to their home from that direction. He got up and opened the door carefully, unsure who he was going to find and came face to face with two men. Theo's immediate response was a wry smile. One was incredibly tall, exaggerating the short stature of the other to comic proportions.

"Uncle Allen!" Daisy jumped up. "Uncle Jack, what happened?"

Of course she could guess what had happened, Nan had called for back up.

Megan remembered Patrick mentioning someone called Allen but she couldn't recall how he fitted into the picture.

Daisy's Uncle Allen reminded Megan of Michelangelo's statue of David – she'd never seen it in real life, but had had the image of it on her wall for a long time after it came on the front of a school prize giving book token. For some reason she'd taken a shine to it. Thankfully, unlike the statue, Allen was wearing clothes. Jack who was as white as a sheet was leaning against Allen trying his best to keep his balance on one leg. His injured foot had been strapped to a splint made from two thick sticks.

"We thought we would have a walk before we came to pick you up," Allen explained. "Jack thought he heard something so went to have a look and stepped on a trap."

"Those bloody poachers," Daisy scowled.

"Daisy, please don't use that kind of language, it's not ladylike!" Allen admonished.

Theo's initial surprise was quickly replaced by doctor-like efficiency. He beckoned them in and drew up a kitchen chair, helping the injured man to sit down.

As soon as Theo's fingers touched Jack, his whole body jerked as though an electric current had gone through it. Pain creased his face and his lips formed an 'oh' but no sound came out. He collapsed, Allen and Theo catching him the best that they could. Even after he hit the floor, his body twisted and turned in ways not normally possible.

Jack's Psychometry had come in handy in his role as a forensic pathologist. It had allowed him to access secrets nobody else would ever know. These secrets helped him to find out why and how people died and he used it to bring the victim and their loved ones justice. You still needed evidence to convict someone – a conversation with a ghost wouldn't stand up in court. Sometimes he would hold onto the histories so he could work on their mysteries at home, making sure no stone was left unturned. This past month had been particularly busy and like sponge he could only hold so much. What with the transformation the night before Jack was drained; his power to block weakened.

When Theo had touched him, he had been unable to block out the mass of history Theo carried him. Now Jack was having a psychic seizure.

It was horrible to see and hear. Cheryl pulled Megan into a protective hug and automatically reached out for Daisy too but she moved quickly out of her reach, going straight to Jack's side.

Daisy placed her hands either side of Jack's head but was careful not to actually touch him. She closed her eyes and Megan understood that she was healing. Allen knelt down and murmured a spell under his breath to increase the strength of his niece's healing energy. They both looked so in control that Theo thought it best not to offer his doctor skills unless of course Jack stopped breathing. It was the first time he had seen a seizure like it. To an untrained eye it might have looked like epilepsy – but not this, this was something entirely different. Theo could understand why people once believed in demonic possession.

What seemed to take hours was in fact only a few seconds. Jack gasped as though someone had plunged him into a bath of ice-water and he began to cough. It was a horrible hacking sound. Only Allen and Daisy saw the large black cloud as it worked its way out of his nose and mouth. As soon as it hit the sunlight streaming through the kitchen window, it dissolved, Jack gave one more cough, and then became still.

Allen and Daisy very slowly took their hands away. Jack was drenched in sweat, shivering and his eyes were closed. Now free from the histories of people who had died, Jack actually looked younger. The soft lines around his eyes were gone, and even the touches of grey in his hair had become less. Allen took off the long woollen coat and placed it gently over him.

"Come on," Cheryl whispered to Megan, "we'll go and check on Tyler and get some blankets."

Megan nodded, glad that she was being given something to do.

"When was the last time he had one of these?" Allen asked Daisy as she gently stroked Jack's damp hair.

"Last month," Daisy said softly. "Work's been really busy."

Jack sat up suddenly and Daisy gave a small squeak of surprise. He was still shaking and didn't seem to be looking at the world. His lips were covered in blood where he had bitten down on his bottom lip. He looked like he'd stepped out of a nightmare.

"I'm sorry… I'm really sorry…" he mumbled. "I've let them down… I've failed… didn't try hard enough…"

"Jack," Allen said softly, "it's alright."

He placed his hand gently onto Jack's arm, and the other man flinched as though he had been burnt.

"No..." he snapped. "No-no-no-no-no.... no sympathy... no kindness... don't deserve it I don't... I wasn't good enough..."

Daisy noticed Theo watching with a frown on his face and she wasn't sure if it was because he was concerned or because he wasn't happy about what he was seeing.

"He's always a bit muddled when he's had a seizure," she said quietly.

Theo nodded though he didn't look very convinced. "Is there anything you'd like me to do?" he asked.

"When he comes round we're going to need a taxi to the hospital, his ankle is definitely broken."

"I can drive you," Theo said. "I'm a doctor there and my parking space is quite close to A & E."

Jack shook his head. He was getting agitated, "I need to get back... there's so much work to be done... can't fail..."

"That will be great, thank you..."

"Theo." Megan's dad offered.

"Thank you, Theo," Allen said.

Cheryl and Daisy walked in with Megan carrying a

blanket.

"Are you okay?" Megan asked kneeling down next to her friend passing the blanket to it.

"Yeah," Daisy whispered placing the blanket around Jack's shoulders. "He's being having these things since I can remember, still makes my insides shake though."

"I'm sorry," Jack mumbled to noone in particular. "That wasn't nice to see."

"Pushing yourself as hard you have done lately probably didn't help matters, Jack." Allen said softly, "That said it's understandable why you have."

"I'll go and bring the car to the front," Theo said heading towards the door.

Daisy stood up, preparing to go along but Allen placed his hand in a stopping motion on her arm. " A&E isn't the nicest place for a child – you really don't need to be there. What will be better, and if it's alright with your friend's Mum, is that you stay here until I can come and get you after I've finished with Jack. It's alright for you to be a child once in a while."

"We'll be happy for you to stay, Daisy," Cheryl said walking over and putting a comforting hand on her shoulder.

"Thank you," Daisy replied although she didn't look

very happy, in fact she looked like she might cry.

Jack looked at Daisy. "Hey, come here." He sounded exhausted. He pulled her into a hug and tussled her hair. "Everything is going to be alright, don't worry okay?" Daisy nodded into his chest. "You don't have to try and mend everyone in one go, little nurse."

Daisy smiled at her nickname and pulled away. "Maybe you should listen to that advice yourself."

Jack smiled and closed his eyes. "I don't mend, I solve – they're two completely different things."

Theo returned from the garage and placed his hand gently onto Jack's arm (ever the doctor with the bedside charm). "Jack we're going to take you to hospital now," he said.

"Okay," Jack sighed. "Just give me a moment to get my act together and…" All at once, with very little effort, Allen picked Jack up into his arms much to Jack's protests.

"Oi, come on, I'm fine, and this isn't doing anything for my masculinity. Hey, I think I'm getting a nosebleed up here."

"Do you seriously think you'll be able to stand?" Allen asked.

"I probably will in a few seconds."

Allen turned to Theo and ignoring Jack said, "Lead the

way please."

Daisy and the others followed them out to the front and watched Allen carefully lower Jack into the front passenger seat. Jack had fallen quiet as soon as they'd gone outside and Daisy wondered how much of him being 'okay' was an act to protect her. As she waved them goodbye, she found herself wishing that she really could mend everyone at once.

17. ALLEN

It would be silly to think that the Bland governments and the other authorities who run the countries of the world don't know that Psychs, Magicks, and Paranaturals exist; they learnt a very long time ago that they are too valuable to get rid of and so they make sure they help them to hide and live undiscovered by those who would panic and try and make war against them.

There are also departments and divisions in governments, military and the police that are actually run by Psychs, Magicks, and Paranaturals – a kind of self-policing policy – and there is a lot to police.

In the Forensics Department, Allen Monroe worked alongside Psychs, Paranaturals and Blands, (it seemed Death was pretty indiscriminating). This was how Allen had come to work on the case investigating a medical research laboratory, linked to illegal experimentations. Rumours were that the laboratory was trying to turn Blands into Psyches, as well as a whole host of other supernatural mutations. When the lab had gotten hold of Jack they must have thought all their Christmases had come at once: a Paranatural with Psyche abilities. Clearly he was viewed as quite an exception to be protected from the brutal and bungling physical experimentation and they'd taken quite a different route: they'd 'educated' him. A far more chilling approach.

Allen had been the youngest on the team, which was why his superior had suggested he work with Jack. Jack had found it very hard to trust anyone but Allen wasn't just anyone and very soon, Jack and Allen became inseparable.

Jack mumbled something in his sleep bringing Allen's attention back to his adoptive brother and his bedroom. Jack's room had been divided into four orderly quarters; a place where he slept (which looked like a very smart hotel room) a study, a laboratory and an art studio.

They'd spent eight hours at the hospital and now Jack was full of medicines to stop his ankle hurting. His ankle was now in a plaster cast.

Allen could hear Una and Theo talking in the hallway. Although he had tried to be grateful that Theo had stayed with them in order to give them a lift home, he had wished that the doctor had just left them. The doctor's presence had appeared to make Jack on edge

Una saw Theo out with a smile and a small wave but her acts of friendliness disguised disquiet. "There's something about that man that I don't like," she announced as she walked back into the room. "I can't quite put my finger on what it is but it definitely rubs me up the wrong way!"

"He said he would bring Daisy home," Allen said. "Did he let you know when that will be?"

"She'll no doubt be in his car as soon as it's in the driveway," Una replied. "You know what a little nurse she is."

From the corner of the room, Jack mumbled through his drug-induced sleep, "It won't grow if it's kept in the cage all the time."

Una looked at him and sighed. "Bless him! Help me get him into his pyjamas and into bed."

"There's nothing more embarrassing for a grown man than to wake up and find someone has undressed him," Allen replied smiling.

"Don't look." Jack muttered "They won't see you if you don't pay attention to them."

"Of course if I had my magic I'd be able to help him more." Una said sadly.

Allen gave her a sympathetic nod of the head.

She coughed before broaching an awkward point, "Maybe if you had a word with the authorities I'd be..."

"We've already been through this," Allen interrupted. "The authorities didn't take away your abilities; if they had they would have told you so – just like they told you that if you ever put a step wrong you'd go to prison."

Una flinched under his words. They weren't meant to be cruel; they were Allen's way of being protective. She had no right to feel upset. The only reason Una wasn't in prison now was because the judge at her trail had been sympathetic to the orphaned Daisy's plight. The Judge's parting words had cut her deep and still haunted her now. "You're being punished by a higher force and they don't have to explain their reasons – you already know."

"My mind is wide open," Jack murmured. "Give a little pit-a-pat on my shoulder. Give a little pit-a-pat on my shoulder. Give a little pit-a-pat on my shoulder, you shall be my master."

"Those monsters would never have admitted to what they had done if I hadn't cursed them." Una protested. "They killed Brenda and John, and if it hadn't been for Jack, Daisy would have died too. As it is they're both scarred for life."

"They thought the house was empty," Allen reminded her.

"That doesn't make it alright," Una snapped. "I did what any mother would have done; I got justice for my daughter and my granddaughter. I did it out of love. I shouldn't be punished for it."

"You don't know that they wouldn't have come forward. For all you know someone would have turned them in," Allen said. "You know that there are some people who think it was Daisy who cursed them. They're afraid of her you know? You not only hurt those boys, you also hurt Daisy when you did what you did. She's not stupid, she understands what's being said and it hurts her. As for Jack and Dad..."

"What? You blame me for how your Dad is?" Una asked, hurt.

"Something is knocking... knocking..." Jack frowned, balling his hands into tight fists as he started to shake. "And someone is going to answer and let the nightmares in..." he whimpered. "Please don't let them come, please don't let them, please, please, please..."

"Jack," Allen called, knowing not to get too close. The first time he had tried to wake Jack from a nightmare he'd got punched across the face – not deliberately of course but that didn't make it hurt any less.

"Jack wake up."

Jack jumped awake gasping. "Dr. Webb... He wants to put Patrick in a home." His words rushed out in a panic. "He thinks we won't care for him properly because he thinks what we can do isn't real. He thinks it is mumbo jumbo."

"That's why I had a funny feeling about him," Una said.

"It's alright," Allen soothed. "Dad isn't going anyway. We won't let him go anywhere. You were having a bad dream, which is hardly surprising considering what you've been through. Lie back down."

Jack shook his head. "I'm fine now," he replied. "I need to go to work. I've lost a lot of histories tonight and I hadn't finished with them."

"You're not going anywhere," Allen said.

Jack flashed him a dirty look before swinging his legs over the side of the bed. "You're not talking to one to your suspects now, Detective Sergeant. You can hardly put me under house arrest. These are important cases and I can't let any stone left unturned."

"Knowing you, you've turned over every single stone several times and picked them clean," Allen replied hoping flattery might calm Jack's ire.

"I've been thorough but that doesn't mean I haven't missed something. I'm not perfect." Jack looked around for the crutches the hospital had given him.

"You've done enough to make sure justice will be done," Allen said gently.

He knew why Jack was acting the way he was. Jack felt a duty to the living to let them know what had happened to those they loved. The bodies of those who'd died in the laboratory experimentations were never found. Their families would feel the pain of not knowing what had happened to them forever. They had no place to grieve for them – just like Jack had no place grieve his Dad. Of course Jack knew his Dad had passed over, that he was safe, but there were times where he just needed to be physically close to him.

Something drifted across Jack's aura catching Allen's attention.

"What was that?" Allen asked.

"What?" Jack asked using the furniture to pull himself up. He was tired despite having been asleep. His whole body hurt after the episode; his ankle hurt like Hell, and being told he couldn't leave made him feel like a prisoner.

"You know what you've done," Allen said catching

hold of the strange thing that looked like a fluffy grey cloud. He couldn't pull it away from the rest of Jack's aura and Allen felt a deep unease.

"What is it?" Una asked.

"He took Daisy's worry when he hugged her. Even though he was too weak."

"I had too. It was my fault. There's bound to be consequences for what I did," Jack said. "For what *it* did."

Allen pushed him back down into his seat effortlessly and kept his hands on Jack's shoulders. Una's face crumpled with confusion.

"And what did you and the wolf do?" Allen asked softly.

"You know bloody well what *it* did," Jack snapped. "I'm sorry... I should have known the wolf would miss Daisy last night. It was bound to try and find her. He feels very protective of her. I should have locked myself up."

"No you shouldn't," Allen said. "It wasn't your fault and it wasn't the wolf's – you need to let it go."

Jack shook his head. He wanted to push Allen away especially when he started to whisper a spell, but he didn't: Jack didn't want to hurt anyone.

When he'd been at The Place Laboratories they punished him by hurting others. They knew that was the way to hurt him the most. Their pain had been unimaginable but he had managed to take it away from them; to lessen it. Even when he thought he couldn't take anymore, there was always space for more. Like love, pain was borderless.

Maybe, if I could solve one of Allen's cases for him," he thought, *"he would understand why using my ability isn't a bad thing.* Allen still had his hands on Jack's shoulders. *There must be lots of unsolved cases Allen had touched,* Jack thought. Using his psychic abilities, Jack reached out to absorb all the he could but he literally bounced back hard in his seat when he hit a blank wall of magic. Frustrated, Jack pushed against it with all his might, ignoring the spell Allen wrapped around himself.

Allen had surrounded himself with calm and warmth. He could see Jack's frustration getting stronger as he mentally and psychically threw himself against the wall. Allen knew it would stand firm; Jack was too hurt and exhausted to break through. But that wouldn't stop him going until he'd hurt himself. Allen removed his hands, breaking the spell but Jack grabbed hold of his wrists. Small trickles of blood came from each nostril. Allen focused the calm and wrapped it closer around them.

"Jack," he said, "it's time to stop now. Come on, don't

do this to yourself."

Jack shook his head. He had an ability that was his duty to use.

"Personal welfare is of no concern when others are suffering," Jack responded through gritted teeth

He couldn't remember who had taught him that, but it was right, wasn't it?

They remained locked like this for many minutes but Jack's weakened state was no real match against Allen's powers and his eyelids slowly dropped.

"I think he's asleep," Una whispered. "Bless him, he really put up a fight didn't he?"

"Doesn't he always?" Allen responded before whispering, "'Personal welfare is of no concern when others are suffering.'"

With a great deal of gentleness Allen manoeuvred Jack into bed. Jack made a soft noise of protest at being moved but Allen shushed him and stroked his hair. Una tucked the blankets around him to keep him safe. Allen watched his Mum silently, feeling irritation beginning to rise. He had always told her that he should be called if Jack showed any signs of his old ways, one of them becoming obsessional about solving crimes. Allen hadn't expected to be called to retrieve Jack from a trap. Alright it wasn't Una's fault, but

Jack had clearly been wound up as tight an elastic band for too long and he should have been called to come and nip the situation in the bud. It was also affecting Daisy. Una didn't seem to realise this.

Allen turned to her. Now was as good a time to talk as any. "Two nights after the fire, Jack told me about the day Brenda and John came to you about their plans to reveal the existence of Witches to the Blands. He had caught that infection and I don't think he would have told me if it hadn't been for that fever. He would have known it would make me angry with you and Dad, and you know how he feels about families being angry with each other." Allen sat down on the chair next to Jack's bed. "He said he felt the time wasn't right, remember he felt uncomfortable, said it was like an itch deep in his brain mixed up with the feeling you get when you've forgotten something really important. You told him it was going to bring a change to the order to things and that always felt odd."

"Because that's what I thought it was," Una protested quietly. "Jack isn't a clairvoyant, and even if he was, you know that they can only see one possible future."

"Jack is a Paranatural; he's not completely human even when he looks it," he said. "And it's well known that sometimes they get 'feelings' about things, like animals know when a storm is coming. You chose not to listen because you wanted the Blands to know about us but you didn't have the courage to do it yourself. Of course you didn't know how things would turn out – if you'd had that ability you would have talked Brenda out of it. She would have listened to you."

"You know what she was like when she put her mind to something." Una protested, "And if I hadn't agreed with her she would have lost her temper and I would have lost contact with Daisy for goodness knows how many months."

Una had given birth to Brenda just an hour before her brother-in-law's wife had given birth to John. As they grew up their parents had joked that they were more like twins than second cousins; they went to the same school and were best friends but would sometimes fight like cat and dog. Their friendship grew into love, which was sometimes just as fiery as their friendship. Although it isn't against the law for cousins to marry, Una didn't think that family should marry each other. There was something just not right about it. She told Brenda this and they argued about it frequently. Brenda refused to listen, and not wanting to fall out with her daughter forever, Una had begrudgingly accepted her choice.

"I don't know why you feel the need to be so hard on me today, Allen. You're very angry, and I understand that, but I don't think you're being very kind – or fair.

Allen took in a deep breath and let it out slowly. "I don't blame you for what happened to Dad. I don't think his stroke or his dementia are punishment for what you did to those boys," he said. "Taking away your magic was enough punishment, but I do blame you for the guilt Jack feels. I blame you for Daisy getting hurt every time she hears people whisper about her – and if I'm honest I blame you because you can't use magic to relieve some of Dad's suffering."

Allen looked up at Una long enough to see her aura change to dark blue as his words affected her. Satisfied that he'd hurt her enough, he looked away.

18. A CRY IN THE GARDEN.

Megan and Daisy sat in Megan's art studio modelling clay. Megan had showed her friend how to shape the clay and make a pattern on it with a knife. Daisy was making an owl; there were little streaks of clay on her face. Megan was impressed with the owl; its wings were outstretched as if it was ready to take flight.

"It's very good," she said, hoping Daisy could tell she really meant it and wasn't saying it just to be nice.

"Thanks." Daisy gave her a smile. "It's meant to be a barn owl." She looked around the studio. It was full of Megan's artwork. "These are brilliant. You know there are shops in town that would love these sorts of things; you should go and ask them if they could sell some of your work. I don't think they'll say no." She looked back at her owl. "I'm sorry about what happened this morning."

"It wasn't anyone's fault," Megan said quietly. "We had a boy at my old school called Richard who had epilepsy; he could have a seizure at any time. He didn't know when it was going to happen. It was scary the first time but when it kept happening I was still worried about him but not scared." She looked Daisy who looked like she could sleep for a week. "It didn't look like the sort of seizure Richard had, but then I guess they're all different aren't they?"

"Uncle Jack has Psychic Epilepsy," Daisy told her. "Remember I told you he was born a Psyche? Well his ability is Psychometry. If he touches an object or a person he can see what happened to them in their past. He uses it a lot in his job, so he can help find out a lot quicker why someone has died. Sometimes he doesn't let go of the histories because he wants to make sure he hasn't missed anything, and like a sponge, he can only hold onto so much before some starts to leak out."

Megan wished she hadn't mentioned it as Daisy looked sadder than she did.

"Don't feel sorry for me, Megan," Daisy said gently. "There are people who have a much harder life than me."

"Daisy," Cheryl's voice called up the stairs, "Theo's back if you are ready to go home?"

Daisy stood up. "I'll see you at school. Thanks for having me."

Megan nodded because she really didn't know what else to say.

When Daisy had left, Megan went out into the garden with her sketchbook. She needed to think about everything that had happened to her, but there were so many thoughts rushing round her head she needed to slow them down; she always found drawing helped her do this.

She had taken a plastic bag so she could sit on it and not get damp. After much scanning of the garden, she decided on the subject of one of the small angel statues.

Megan made herself comfortable, opened her book, and then froze. She could hear crying. It sounded just like the same crying she'd heard the night she'd gone looking for Daisy. At that time she'd put it down to being spooked by the dark, but now it was daytime and the birds singing. Megan was absolutely sure it was coming from the other side of the hedge.

She got up, picking up her bag and sketchbook and moved closer to the hedge. The branches were thick but bare because of winter, and Megan found if she went up close to it, she could see right into the hotel gardens (which looked very grand, with huge topiary animals, stalking their way across a tidy lawn) At this time of year the flower-beds were empty, and she could see right over to the large pond.

Sat at the pond-side was a little girl who had her face in her hands. Megan could see from the rise and fall of her shoulders that she was crying.

Megan wasn't good at guessing ages but she was certain that she was no older than six. She was small and her blonde hair was tied up into piggy tails. She was wearing a pink dress with thin shoulder straps and white sandals, clearly dressed for summer. She didn't seem bothered by the icy air nipping at her face. Megan knew instinctively that she was looking at a ghost. She took a deep breath and held back tears. Of course children died, she knew that, but it didn't make seeing a child ghost any easier, especially when she was so sad as well.

"Hello," she called.

The girl looked up, she was certainly a cute little thing, with a round face, and dark brown eyes. Tears streamed down her face, and she wiped them away with her hand. She looked around to see where the voice had come from and saw Megan peering out from the branches, giving off a very soft glow.

"Where's that light coming from?" she asked.

Megan didn't think it was a good idea to tell her about how only ghosts, spirits, and others who belong to the supernatural and paranormal world could see the light she was talking about; she didn't want to scare her, and even though she read some of the book which Daisy had given her, she didn't think she would be able to explain it very well.

"I'll tell you about that soon," Megan replied. "Why are you crying?"

The little girl's bottom lip wobbled, "I can't find my Mummy." She started to cry again.

"Please, don't cry," Megan said gently. "When was the last time you saw her?"

"I don't remember," the little girl sobbed. "She always says that if I ever get lost then I should stay right where I am and she will come and find me. It feels like she's been gone for a very long time."

Megan found tears pricking her own eyes when she started to wonder how long this little girl had been waiting for her Mummy to come.

"What's your name?" Megan asked.

The little girl looked worried and looked around nervously. "I'm not supposed to talk to people I don't know."

"My name is Megan," Megan told her gently, "and I want to help you find your Mummy, but I can't really do that if I don't know what your name."

"India Coles," the little girl answered.

"Okay, India," Megan said kindly. "When I've lost something I try and think very hard where I saw it last. Can you remember when you saw your Mummy last?"

Megan thought that if she made the little girl aware it was winter she'd realise that the last time she saw her Mummy was summer. Hopefully then she could help her realise something was very wrong, and then Megan could gently break it to her that she was in fact a ghost.

"Mummy and Daddy were having a drink over there," India said pointing to inside the hotel. "Zoe was having a swim, and Luke was talking to some boys."

"Who are Zoe and Luke?" Megan asked.

"My big brother and sister," India said. "They didn't want to come here but Mummy said they had to."

"And what were you doing?" Megan asked. She wanted to know why India's brother and sister didn't want to come to the hotel but she was afraid of delaying the painful situation longer.

"I was playing with my ball," India told her, "but I dropped it in the water."

Megan found her stomach twist into knots at the thought of this poor little girl falling into the water and not being able to get out. She knew it was important for India to remember what had happened to her but the thought of her remembering her death upset her.

"And did you try and get it?" Megan asked.

India nodded. "I fell in," she frowned, "but I really don't remember how I got out."

Megan remembered her Mum saying you only have to take your eyes off a child for a second for something to happen. When it came to children it was like destiny had its own plan.

Megan thought hard. She knew she needed to help India cross over, but how she was going to do that when she thought her Mummy was going to come and get her.

"India," Megan said softly, "do you know what dead is?"

India nodded. "My hamster died," she said looking sad as she remembered. "His name was Nibbles. Zoe said he was very old for a hamster. She said that when someone gets really old their body stops working, like when Daddy's watch got old. The things inside couldn't work anymore, so everything stopped. Zoe said that when someone's body dies, their soul comes out of their body and they go to heaven like Nanny did."

"Do you know what a soul is?" Megan asked.

"Yes Zoe told me. It's what makes you a person."

Megan began to feel hopeful that if India knew about souls then maybe it would be easier to tell her that she was a ghost.

"India, has anyone come to talk to you whilst you've been waiting for Mummy?"

"I saw Nanny," India told her, "but she's in heaven so I must have fallen asleep and dreamt it."

Megan took a deep breath, it was clear there was going to be no gentle way to make India realise she was a ghost. Megan took a deep breath and hoped it would all go better than she feared.

"Okay, Zoe was right about Nibbles getting old and his body not working anymore," she said, "but sometimes that's not why people die, sometimes their body gets really sick and can't get better, and then sometimes their body gets broken so badly that it can't fix itself."

"Like when you wind up a toy too much?"

"That's right." Megan nodded. "Do you know what a caterpillar changes into?"

"We learnt about in school." She frowned. "Why are you asking me all these questions? I thought you were going to help me find my Mummy."

"India, I need to tell you something," Megan employed the same tone of voice her Mum used when Tyler had hurt himself. It always seemed to calm him down. "I need to tell you why you can't find your Mummy. India I'm really, really sorry but the reason why you don't remember getting out of the pond is because you didn't. Your body filled up with water and broke, that's why you saw your Nanny, you weren't dreaming, she'd come to take you to heaven."

India's eyes filled with tears. "No, you're lying! You don't want to help me find my Mummy. Go away!"

"I'm not lying," Megan said. "India, please, listen to me. I can see ghosts and spirits and..."

"That's why you're glowing!" India gasped. "You're the ghost and you want me to think I'm a ghost too so I go away with you. You want to take me away from my Mummy."

"No, I don't India, please..."

"Go away!" India screamed. "Leave me alone! Mummy! Mummy! I want my Mummy!"

Megan crawled away from the hedge feeling hot tears running down her face. What had she done? There was no way India was going to believe anything she said. India was going to wait by that pond waiting for her Mummy to come. Only she wouldn't be coming. Not for a very, very, long time.

Megan wiped her eyes with the sleeve of her coat.

There was no way she was going to let that happen.

19. SCOTT'S HOUSE.

Scott put another heaped tablespoon of sugar onto his second helping of cornflakes before placing a large spoonful into his mouth. His Mum was making his packed lunch and he could see lots of homemade goodies going in, which made him lick his lips. Anna Brown (she went back to her maiden name after she divorced Scott's Dad) was a fantastic cook, and she worked hard in the care home, where she worked part time, to make sure the residents got whatever meals they wanted even though it was often hard because the home had a budget to keep to. She was six foot and muscular. Her brown hair was always tied up into a bun, which made her square face look hard. On first meeting, people either thought she was a man wearing a dress or that she was likely to thump them for no reason. This was unfair really because Anna was one of the gentlest, kindest people you could ever meet.

"Mum, can Megan and Daisy come round for tea

tonight?" Scott asked making sure that he'd swallowed the mouthful of cereal before he spoke. Anna hated it when anyone spoke with their mouth full. Nothing was too important to say with a full mouth.

"If it's alright with whoever looks after them I don't see why not." Anna replied turning around and giving Scott a smile. She had met Megan briefly when she had dropped Scott off for tea at Stone Towers. She had seemed like a nice girl and Scott had told Anna a lot about her – especially about the day Tim and April had said they'd not be his friends if he stayed friends with Megan and Daisy. To be honest, Anna was hopeful that they'd stick to their threat. She had only tolerated them because they seemed to be Scott's friends. In her opinion, Tim was a little full of himself, clearly thinking himself cleverer than he really was, and April, well after Anna had overheard her ask Scott if she was Scott's uncle, she hadn't had the warmest feelings towards the girl. Anna had only seen Daisy from a distance, when she had left Scott at the school gates. Of course she had heard a lot about her from Scott, and the town gossips, but as a rule she chose not to listen to the gossips. How anyone could be scared of a little girl? Alright the little girl was a Witch, but everyone knew they had rules they had to go by; the main one being, 'do what you will but harm none'. Every time she saw Daisy sitting under the tree in the playground reading, or drawing in the dirt with a stick, she felt the irrational desire to go over and give her hug.

Scott's siblings, Bethany and Liam walked into the kitchen. Bethany was tall and slender, and unlike her Mum, there was no way to mistake her for a man; she resembled a plastic fashion doll, only her eyes held more warmth, and her smile was more genuine.

"You're going out again?" Bethany teased her younger brother. "You've got more of a social life than me."

"At least he doesn't have to carry a stake around with him when he goes out," Liam replied snatching up the packet of cornflakes before Bethany could get to them. She rolled her eyes and sat opposite him.

"That was just once." Bethany reminded him, "How was I to know he was a vampire? The vampire look was in then, remember? It was very hard to tell the difference. Why do you insist on bringing it up? "

Anna replied for him. "Because it annoys you. Don't pay any attention to it and he'll stop." She looked at Liam, who was also tall and built like a whippet with his narrow face and sharp nose. "And you, Mister, leave her alone; it's done, it's over, time to move on. You going on about it is just boring, and it's starting to annoy me."

"If it had happened to me I'd never have heard the last of it," Liam muttered pouring milk over his cornflakes. "Which one of them girls is your girlfriend then Scott?"

"Neither of them," Scott replied, blushing. "We're just friends."

"I bet its Megan," Liam said. "I mean that Witch girl isn't the best looking, is she?" Liam's smirk quickly turned into a grimace. "OW! Mum, Scott kicked me!"

"That wasn't Scott," Bethany replied. "God, Liam, what's gotten into you? You weren't always such a turd."

"I'm not staying here to be insulted," Liam announced standing up. "I'm going to school."

"Liam, wait. Sit down and have breakfast," Anna begged she looked at her daughter. "Bethany apologise."

"Me?" Bethany frowned. "I'm not the one being rude about Scott's friend." She glared at her brother. "Some yobs burnt down her house remember? Her parents were killed and she was hurt so badly she nearly died! How can you make fun of the way she looks?"

"I'll get breakfast from the shop," he said to Anna as he walked out of the kitchen.

"Mum, you need to find out what the hell is going on with him," Bethany protested. "He's going to grow up like…" She nearly said Dad but remembered quickly how that would affect Scott, "…a jerk."

Anna turned her attention to Scott. "Sweetheart, you've got milk on your tie. Go and get your spare."

Scott knew Mum wanted to talk to Bethany alone. He wanted to tell her that he wasn't a baby anymore. He needed to know what was happening. Liam was his brother and he was worried about him. Sighing he left the kitchen. This morning wasn't the time to have the battle; and he really had spilt an awful lot of milk on his tie.

"It's not drugs is it?" Bethany asked worried.

"No, no nothing like that," Anna said sitting down. "Liam is struggling with his school work. I mean really struggling. They want to have his assessed for learning difficulties .We were meant to have a meeting with the SEN-Co, Mr. Clark."

"And when you say 'we' you mean you, Liam and Dad? Let me guess again, Dad didn't turn up."

"I guess he thinks being that Dad can't be bothered to care anymore, than why should he?" Anna sighed. "I've tried to talk to him but I can't reach him."

Bethany took hold of her Mum's hand wishing she knew what to say. Instead she found herself looking at Scott's breakfast bowl.

"Mum, I think you need to seriously talk to Scott about cutting down how many cornflakes he has with his sugar."

Anna looked down and burst out laughing for the first time in a long time.

20. PROBLEMS SHARED.

Daisy sat under her favourite tree drawing spirals in the dirt with a stick. She was tired and sad, and really wished her Mum was around to give her a hug. Patrick was spending more and more time sleeping. He looked awful with his mouth wide open and his cheekbones sticking. The weight was falling off him, and he didn't call her Brenda anymore. He would politely call her 'dear'. Daisy wondered how long it would be before he forgot who Nan was. A stray tear ran down her cheek and she wiped it away angrily. Stop it, she scolded herself, crying wouldn't bring him back, just as crying didn't bring her parents back. A sudden memory of confusion and annoyance hit her. She knew it didn't belong to her and it caused her to look up and see Scott making his way across the playground. She took a deep breath, let it out slowly and went to meet him halfway.

"What's wrong?" she asked. "You're upset."

"My brother Liam is being a jerk and Mum and Bethany are shutting me out." Scott sighed heavily. "The whole family treats me like a baby, as if I can't handle anything serious."

Daisy gave him a kind look. "Maybe it's hormones."

"I don't think so," Scott shook his head. "Mum made me leave the room so she could talk to Bethany about it. I don't think she'd want to talk to my sister about Liam's hormones, do you?"

"No," Daisy agreed. "If there was something really dreadful then I'm sure your Mum would have warned you. She probably doesn't want you to know what's going on because there's nothing you can do There's nothing worse than knowing something and not being able to help."

"But she told Bethany," Scott protested.

"How old is Bethany?"

"She's sixteen."

"Well, she's nearly an adult then isn't she? Sometimes adults need to talk to other adults just to get their feelings out, like what you're doing with me now," Daisy replied. "There are some things only kids can talk to kids about because only they will understand, and there are some things that only adults can talk to adults about because only they will understand. Sometimes an adult has to tell a kid something that makes them grow up pretty quickly, and believe me, that's no fun at all."

For the first time that morning Scott really looked at Daisy and he saw that she was paler than usual. Dark rings circled her eyes. Clearly she hadn't got much sleep.

"Daisy, what's happened?" He put his hand gently on her arm.

"Don't." Daisy said quietly though not unkindly. She took a step away from him. "If you're nice, I'm going to cry."

"There's nothing wrong with that."

Daisy smiled sadly. "Yeah, well for others maybe, but not for me." She cleared her throat. "My Granddad... he isn't doing too good at the moment, and it's making my Nan sad. There's nothing I can do to help."

"Is he in hospital?" Scott asked.

"No. There's nothing they'd be able to do anyway." Daisy pulled at a piece of thread hanging from her coat sleeve. "He's better off at home rather than surrounded by... strangers." A sad thought hit her. "At least we love him. I think he can feel that."

"Daisy... I don't know what to say."

"There's nothing you can say." The thread came off in her hand and she let it drop, watching it as it floated to the ground. "It's part of life, people get sick and then they die." She shrugged. "It doesn't stop it from sucking big time. It doesn't stop you from being sad."

"Wouldn't it be better if you were at home?" Scott asked.

Daisy shook her head. "This probably sounds really horrible but I need a break. Life's a bit crazy. It isn't just Granddad. Uncle Jack's injured his leg. He stood on an animal trap. The shock of it gave him a seizure. It all happened when they were coming to pick me up from Megan's."

"Good job her Dad is a doctor," Scott offered. Daisy pulled a face. "What?"

"You know those stones I gave Megan's Mum for Tyler's asthma?" Scott nodded. "Well, he thinks it's mumbo jumbo. He's a scientist and doesn't believe in that sort of thing. He thinks my family relies on herbs and charms and he only came to my house to see if we were looking after Granddad properly."

"Is your uncle okay?"

"He's had seizures before."

"So you didn't have a good weekend then?" Scott said offering a sympathetic smile.

"There were some good bits. I enjoyed spending time

with you and Megan," she said. "And the sleepover was fun and…" her happy babble was cut off, "Uh oh."

Scott looked at her worried, "Uh oh?"

"Megan is coming and she's worried." Daisy looked across the playground. "What on Earth is going on today? It's not even a full moon."

"What's that got to do with it?" Scott asked.

"Full moons have an effect on how people are feeling. We'll talk about it later," Daisy said walking over to meet Megan. "What's happened?"

Megan had planned on what she was going to say to Daisy and Scott all the way to school, she had been so quiet in the car that her Mum had asked her if there was something bothering her. Megan had told her that it was because they were going to play netball in P.E. Megan wasn't good at sports and was often picked last, so it was natural for her to be worried. Her mum was happy to believe that was the height of her daughter's troubles. Megan wished she could tell her Mum what was really going on but what if she thought she was making up stories to get attention, or worse that she thought she had gone completely round the bend and took her to the doctors.

Daisy looked exhausted and Megan thought how unfair it was to keep unloading her problems onto her friend.

"Hello Scott."

He offered a little wave and smile in return.

Megan turned her attention to Daisy. "How's your Uncle Jack?"

Scott didn't look excited so Megan guessed Daisy had stuck to her decision not to tell Scott about the whole werewolf thing.

"He's driving me up the wall. He hates being cooped up indoors," Daisy replied. "Now could you answer my question; I felt you worrying before you even came through the gates."

"It's something I should probably work out for myself," Megan said. "Don't worry about it."

"Is 'it' about ghosts?" Daisy asked. When Megan couldn't think up of a lie quickly enough Daisy nodded. "Okay, have you talked to Tabitha about it? That's her job after all."

Megan looked uncomfortable and looked away. Megan hated to admit it, but she and Tabitha had drifted apart in the last few days. Megan wasn't entirely sure that they were a compatible pair of associates.

"She hasn't said something to upset you has she," Scott asked.

"No," Megan said quietly. "She's okay. It's... I

haven't actually called her…"

They both looked at Megan sharply and she squirmed under their scrutiny. "I didn't call her when I probably should have."

"You tried to help a ghost on your own?" Daisy asked lowering her voice so that no one nearby could hear her. Megan nodded. "Didn't you read the book I gave you?"

"I did but I thought I could do it on my own," Megan replied. "I couldn't. I really, I mean *really*, messed it up. Which is why I don't want to talk to Tabitha as she's going to be really mad with me." She sighed sadly. "*I'm* really mad with me."

"Being mad with yourself isn't going to help this ghost," Daisy said. "Why not tell us what happened? Maybe we can help."

Megan looked at Scott, who was doing his best to look encouraging.

"When you left yesterday I went into the garden to do some drawing, and then I heard someone crying from behind the hedge. I looked through the branches and saw the hotel's garden on the other side, and that's where I saw a little girl wearing a summer dress."

"A little girl?" Scott asked.

Megan nodded. "She looked about six. She was by the

pond, and was crying really hard. I asked her what was wrong and she told me that she'd lost her Mummy. I knew it was more like her mummy had lost her. It didn't take much to work out what had happened to her. It's just so sad.

"Poor little mite," Daisy murmured.

Megan carried on her tale, "She told me her name was India. She remembers falling into the water but she doesn't remember getting out."

"So she drowned," Scott said sadly.

Megan nodded. "I asked her if anyone had come to see her whilst she was waiting and she said that she had seen her Nan. I tried to tell her as gently as possible that the reason why she didn't remember getting out of the water was because she didn't. I also tried to tell her that she had really seen her Nan and that she hadn't been dreaming. She didn't believe me. She thought The Glow around me meant I was a ghost and that I was trying to take her away from her Mummy. She just wouldn't listen."

"Why on Earth didn't you call Tabitha?" Daisy asked.

"I thought I'd be able to help her because she's little," Megan said quietly. "I thought she'd trust me because I'm a kid. I made a mistake and now she's probably going to be stuck for a long time and it's all my fault."

"You didn't mean to," Scott said kindly. "She probably wouldn't have listened to anyone."

"I can't just leave her there," Megan said. "What shall I do?"

"School isn't the best place to make plans," Daisy answered. "There are too many people around and I'm not really up to doing a big guarding spell today."

"You can come back to my house after school," Scott said keenly. "I've already asked Mum if you could come for tea. My family is pretty open minded, so if they did overhear anything they won't think too much of it."

"Oh yeah," Daisy said recalling, "didn't your sister date a vampire for a while?" Daisy asked. Scott looked at her in surprise. "Magicks, and Paranaturals have a pretty tight community, someone sneezes in the morning everyone knows about it by the afternoon."

"Yeah, but she really doesn't like anyone talking about it," Scott replied protectively. "She's a bit embarrassed that she didn't notice."

It was Daisy's turn to look surprised. "Pardon? What? How didn't she...?"Daisy's sentence trailed off with Megan's reaction. "Megan are you ok?"

Megan had gone very pale and her eyes had widened with fright. "Vampires?" she whispered. "There are real vampires? Here?"

Daisy silently told herself off. How on earth could she have been so careless; the world of supernatural beings was still new to Megan. Daisy put her arm around her friend.

It was going to be a very long day.

21. BULLIES

Liam Whyman really wished he hadn't told Jacob and Dillon Pitt that his little brother was inviting Daisy home for tea. The twins were large for fourteen year olds, and would have looked more at home on the ruby playing field than a school playground. Their hair was cut short, and they had hard, grey eyes that were always on the lookout for someone weaker than them (which meant pretty much everybody). They'd pick on someone for whatever small thing made them different. Liam didn't really like them, but his role of the school clown, (which hid the struggle he fought in every class except for sports) made the Pitt twins laugh. This meant they liked him. This meant they left him alone.

He had been angry about breakfast and the words had just come out. Before he'd had a chance to take them back, the cold wind had blown across the playground had whipped them away. The Pitt twins didn't believe Daisy was a Witch with special powers, and they thought up many cruel things in order to try and make her cry. Liam didn't want to make anyone cry, especially a girl who had been hurt in a fire that had killed her parents, and he didn't really want to upset his brother – after all, as annoying as he was, he did love him

But as soon as he'd opened his mouth, he'd set about a chain-reaction that couldn't be stopped. The Pitt Twins had insisted on him going along with them at the end of the school and Liam found he had little choice it was his job to collect Scott from wherever he was in school and he knew he would be with Daisy and Megan. Liam took a deep breath and hoped that Scott would forgive him.

Daisy turned around and looked at Liam, stopping him before the taunts could start. "No, I don't have cloven feet," she said. "I don't sacrifice animals, dance naked it the moonlight or ride a broomstick. No it wasn't careless of me to lose my Mum and Dad, I got these burns trying to get to my parents room. Yes my skin burnt and of course it bloody hurt. Yes I did cry and no, I didn't curse those boys to make their skin burn."

Liam felt his mouth go dry; she had answered everything The Pitt Twins had told him to ask.

"Erm..." was all he muttered. He looked at Dillon and

Jacob for support.

"Do mirrors crack when you look at them?" Dillon asked grinning.

"I'm surprised we haven't all turned to stone just looking at you," Jacob chimed in.

Scott looked at his brother, "Liam?"

His brother looked away with shame and Scott thought that he'd never hated his brother as much as he did in that moment.

"Have you finished?" Daisy asked.

Jacob shook his head. "You think you're so great, don't you?" sneered Jacob.

"No, not really," Daisy answered.

Dillon sniggered, "What are you going to do? Turn us into toads?"

"Even if she could, she wouldn't," Megan said angrily. "Look, she hasn't done anything to you. She's not said anything to you, so please just leave her alone."

Jacob glared at her. "And what the hell are *you* supposed to be?" he demanded. "Dillon look at this *thing* – someone's shaved a poodle and put it in a school uniform."

"Don't!" Daisy said.

"Don't? Poodle here just said you can't do anything to us," Jacob reminded her.

"Don't be like your Dad," Daisy sneered looking at the twins. "He's a bully too, isn't he?"

"No," Jacob scowled. "Shut up, you don't know anything about our Dad!"

"Yes I do," Daisy replied. "The wind heard what you were going to do today, you were going to see if you could make a Witch cry. The wind told the birds, who went to your home – where a dog was chained up in a backyard full of junk."

"Everyone knows where we live," Jacob said. "Nice try."

"Your Dad hits your Mum." Daisy's eyes had narrowed and hardened. She seemed completely aware of the blows she was delivering and Megan flinched. "She gets hit when she hasn't done his dinner right. She gets hit if she irons the wrong shirt for work. She gets hit when he's drunk. He tells her that she's useless and that he puts up with her. He says that she's so ugly no one else would want her." Daisy took a step forward. "And she believes him. Your Dad is bigger than both of you – stronger – if you tried to stop him, he could hold one brother away with one hand whilst he's beat the other."

"Shut up!" Dillon snapped. Tears were in his eyes.

"That's why you two are bullies," Daisy said sadly.

"Because you've been bullied by your Dad for so long that you think the bigger bully you are, the more you get what you want. You think that people will give into you out of fear. You're both growing up to be like your Dad, and your Mum can see it. It's breaking her heart."

"Dillon told you to shut up!" Jacob shouted, getting the attention of those around them. Daisy stepped forward, ignoring the threat and Dillon punched her. Hard.

"Daisy!" Megan shouted running to her friend's side.

"What is wrong with you?" Liam demanded, standing in front of Daisy so neither Dillon nor Jacob to get to her. "She's only twelve! And she's a girl!"

"Are you alright?" Scott crouched down next to her.

"I'm going to have one hell of a black eye," Daisy muttered.

Everything happened all at once; people gathered around them, some were shouting at Dillon and Jacob about hitting a girl half the size of them, a few bent down to help Daisy thinking she was in shock because she wasn't crying, and others stood and stared, waiting for something Witchy to happen. They were actually disappointed when nothing did. Ravendale's head teacher, Mrs Kenley came marching out to see what had caused the commotion.

"Scott, go and get Granddad," Liam said. Knowing

that their grandfather would be waiting in his car for them outside the school gates.

"You go and get Granddad," Scott replied angrily. "I'm staying with Daisy."

"What on earth is going on here?" Mrs Kenley voice rose up above everyone.

As all attention turned to her, Dillon and Jacob used the opportunity to run. Everyone talked at once. Megan helped Daisy to her feet. Her eye was starting to swell shut and bruise horribly.

Mrs Kenley was a tall, spindly woman, with sharp cheekbones and a hooked nose; she was pale and had thin, blond hair cut into a bob. As soon as saw Daisy's eye she placed a comforting hand onto the girl's shoulder.

"We had better get you something cold to put on that," she said gently. "Scott and... Megan isn't it? You had better come to," she said nodding to Liam and Scott.

"Our Granddad is waiting for us." Liam told her.

"Could you go and get him please," Mrs Kenly replied. "We'll be in my office." She turned her attention back to Daisy, "We'd best call your Nan and let her know what has happened."

Reg Brown, Liam and Scott's grandfather, wasn't an

overly handsome man; he wouldn't make anyone look twice if they past him in the street, but he did have a pleasant friendly face. He was of medium height and size although he was getting a little potbelly. His thick grey hair was untidy and he wore glasses, which perched on the end of his turned up nose. His hazel eyes often sparkled whenever something caught his interest. However, sitting in Mrs Kenley's office, his eyes weren't sparkling. He listened to Liam tell the Head about how the Pitt Twins wanted to make Daisy cry and how he'd gone along with it. Daisy sat with a cool-pack over her bruised eye, and Una sat next to her clearly angry that someone had hit her granddaughter. Liam explained that Daisy had wound Dillon up by talking about their dad hitting their mum. Mrs Kenley shifted uncomfortably.

"Do you know for certain Daisy that Mrs Pitt is being hit by Mr Pitt?" Mrs Kenley asked.

"Everybody knows that," Daisy replied looking at Mrs Kenley with her one good eye. "I don't understand why no one isn't doing anything about it."

Mrs Kenley nodded. "The adult world is complicated. It probably wasn't a good idea to mention it to Dillon and Jacob."

"I think they know what's going on in their own house,

Mrs Kenley!" Daisy said. "What made them angry was that I pointed out that they were no different to their dad. Then I forgot to duck."

Reg had to quickly disguise a laugh as a cough, but it didn't go unnoticed by Mrs Kenley who shot him a disapproving look.

"You shouldn't be blaming Daisy for getting hit," Una protested. "It should be those two little thugs who came here to pick on her that should be in here, not these children."

"I'm not blaming Daisy, Mrs Monroe," Mrs Kenley replied. "The children are here so I can get a clear picture of what happened. This is after all a very serious matter and to be fair, Daisy isn't entirely innocent in all of this."

Una pouted and adjusted her bag in her lap before turning her attention to Liam. "And do you have anything to say, young man?"

"I'm sorry," he said quietly. He decided that the only way for Scott to forgive him was to tell the truth and hoped he understood, "I'm afraid of Dillon and Jacob, I let them think I'm their friend so they don't pick on me."

"So instead you pick on other people instead?" Una asked icily.

"Nan," Daisy said. "Liam did stand between me and

the boys so they wouldn't be able to do anything else to me."

Reg turned in his seat and looked at Una. Her eyes were glowing, a clear sign that she was furious. He studied her hard. They weren't burning as brightly as they should be and he wondered if it was because she was ill or tired. He'd heard that her husband wasn't very well. Although he was curious, he knew that now wasn't the time or the place to ask.

"I promise that we'll have a serious talk to Liam when we get home," Reg told her. He turned to Mrs Kenley and asked, "Is there anything further we can help you with?"

"No, thank you, that's all," Mrs Kenley replied.

She watched the small group leave her office and sighed. She had never regretted accepting Daisy Monroe into her school; Shirley Kenley had been absolutely disgusted at the reaction of those parents (and some of the staff) at Winterbourne when they had found out Daisy was coming – organising a petition to say they didn't want her because her presence would scare their children. Well, Shirley told herself, Winterbourne had lost out. Daisy was an intelligent and compassionate child, although Shirley had often wished she would play with the other children. She'd never been so pleased as when Daisy had befriended

Megan and Scott. Daisy was right about the Pitt boys – if they kept seeing their bully of a Dad hitting their Mum they would grow up to be just like him. She needed to finally make the call to the authorities. First she had to make herself comfortable; it would be a long conversation. Getting up, she made sure the door of her office was locked and closed the curtains. Satisfied she was alone, she pulled off her hands as though they were gloves, and stretched out her long red claws.

22. WHAT FRIENDS DO.

Scott sat at the dining room table with Megan and Daisy. They only used the dining room on special days like Christmas or birthdays, so it was the perfect place to do homework because it was quiet and there wasn't any television to distract him. The living room was out of bounds at the moment anyway because that was where his Mum and Granddad were talking to Liam. He hoped Liam he was having a hard time of it. He was still angry with him. Daisy had finished her homework and was now helping everybody else. Her Nan had wanted to take her home, but Daisy had pointed out that she was going to have the same black eye at home as at Scott's so she might as well end her day enjoying herself.

Scott closed his Maths book and put it back into his school bag. He hesitated for a minute and then took out another exercise book, with a cover that was dirty from being taken out and rested on picnic tables and often on the school field. The pages were curled at the edges where it had got damp from the bath. He suddenly felt nervous and wondered if he was doing the right thing. What if he upset Daisy by asking her? Or what if she thought it was a stupid idea? What if... ?

"What's wrong?" Daisy asked.

"I've been writing stories," Scott said holding out the book, "about Psyches and Paranaturals, only, the characters are like real Psyches and Paranaturals – you know, not the ones in fairy-tales or horror stories. I thought that people pay more attention to stories so that's why they're good at getting messages across. I thought that if I wrote about them, people would learn that they're not all bad. They would accept them if they ever found out if they were real." He swallowed hard. Had everything he had said made sense? He wasn't sure. "I want to be a writer you see, and... could you read them for me, to check that I haven't got anything wrong?"

"I'd love to," Daisy said taking the book from him. "You know as long as you don't have Witches living in gingerbread houses and eating children you're allowed some artistic leeway."

Megan closed her book with a sigh. Both Scott and Megan had noted that she hadn't paid her schoolwork any attention in over twenty minutes. Tabitha was playing on her mind and it didn't take a Psyche to know that. .

"Have you finished?" Daisy asked.

Megan nodded and put her homework away. "She's going to be so mad at me isn't she?" she asked.

"You're not going to know that unless you call her," Daisy replied.

"You made a mistake," Scott pointed out. "Everyone makes a mistake. And you are kind of new to all of this."

Megan chewed the bottom of her lip and thought as hard as she could about Tabitha.

"Wow," a familiar voice came behind her and Megan startled to discover just how easy it was to summon her. "What or who happened to your mate?" Tabitha asked.

"A bully tried to make her cry and when she stood up to him he punched her in the face," Megan answered.

"When I was at school if a boy hit a girl we called him a jessy!" Tabitha said lighting a cigarette. "It was definitely frowned upon. I'm not saying it didn't happen but..." Tabitha's recollection trailed off and she stubbed out her cigarette against the metal case. "Christ, Megan what's wrong? You're shaking."

"You're going to be so mad at me," Megan whispered.

"Why would I be mad?"

"Because I tried to help a ghost on my own," Megan looked down at her hands not wanting to see the disappointment in her spirit guide's face. "She's a little girl who drowned. I told her she was dead but she didn't believe me. She said that her Nan and talked to her but she thought that it was a dream. She's wearing summer clothes but doesn't seem to realise that it's winter."

"Time doesn't always have any meaning for ghosts," Tabitha said. "What they think happened yesterday actually happened years ago."

"That doesn't really matter when you're really little and you can't find your Mummy; each second feels like years." Megan looked up at Tabitha. "You're not angry that I didn't call you?"

"I'd have probably thought the same thing if I were in your shoes," Tabitha replied, "You must never be afraid to call me. I'm your spirit guide and my job is to help you, not tell you off." She sighed heavily. "There should be a rule that kids shouldn't die. I'm actually annoyed that her Nan didn't stick around and try and convince her to come with her."

"Could you try and find her?" Megan asked hopefully. "Maybe you could talk to her."

"The afterlife is a pretty big place sweetie," Tabitha

said. "And if she thought her Nan was a dream last time then she'll think it's a dream again."

"That's my fault." Megan said.

"No, it's not. It's hard enough to explain about death to children when they're alive. The reason why she won't cross over is because she's waiting for her Mummy. What we need to do is to find her. She must be alive otherwise she would have come and collected India herself by now."

"Maybe we can find her on the internet."

Megan turned to Scott and Daisy who were eagerly waiting for the report back. "Tabitha thinks that if we find India's Mum then we can help her cross over. There must be something on the Internet about her death; it would probably have been quite big news."

"Right!" Scott got up from his chair and went over to the computer in the corner of the dining room. "What did you say her name was?"

"India Cole," Megan answered.

"Does Tabitha have any ideas on how we are going make India's Mum believe that her little girl is haunting Stone Towers?" Daisy asked.

"We've got to convince India she's dead first," Tabitha said. "Let's tackle one problem at a time."

"She thinks we should make India realise she's a ghost

first," Megan offered. Megan wrinkled her nose. The effort of constantly translating was becoming annoying; they were going to have to find a way around it. But not today, they had bigger issues to deal with.

"I've got 115,000,000 results," Scott announced. "Lots are on social websites and..." he clicked on the computer's keys, "one is on one of those ancestry websites and she died in 1883 so it's definitely not her."

"What about Googling 'child drowning in hotel garden'?" Daisy offered.

Scott typed it into the computer and shook his head. "No, there's a lot on pond safety," he said. "I'll type in Stone Towers." He shook his head again. "Nope, just the website."

"The library might have some old local newspapers on their records." Daisy looked at the clock on the wall. "It'll be shut now but we could go and look tomorrow after school."

"It could take ages," Megan warned. "I can't tell what year she died."

"My Uncle Jack could help," Daisy said " and it'll get him out of the house, which would be doing everyone a favour! He could do a psychometric reading and give us an idea of the year."

"Mr Brown, the Hotel Manager, keeps going on about how it would be nice for me to come and look round. I think he wants to get in Mum's good books as he's been calling her to look at paperwork a lot at the moment," Megan said. "We could also try the cream tea they have there."

"The website says the Stone Towers teas are legendary." Scott said his eyes shining at the thought. "If it's alright with you two I can tell Granddad what's going on and he can come with us; he knows a lot about ghosts as well."

Daisy shrugged dismissively. "Well he already knows I'm a Witch. I don't think Uncle Jack will mind if he knew his ability as well, it's probably common knowledge to most of the town anyhow."

"Thanks for helping," Megan said.

"That's what friends do," Daisy reminded her with a smile. "You honestly didn't think we'd let you do this all on your own, did you?"

Megan wasn't exactly sure what she'd been expecting. Anna called out that dinner was ready. Scott and Daisy dashed off to the kitchen. Tabitha looked at Megan sadly causing her to hang back.

"What's wrong?" she asked.

"I just want to warn you," Tabitha said quietly, "even with all our hard work we might not be able to get India to cross over. We might not be able to find her Mum and even if we did there's a really strong chance that she's not going to believe us."

"But that doesn't mean we can't try, right?"

"That's all we can do," Tabitha replied. "Just remember that's what we did, we tried."

Megan nodded and went to join her friends, hoping that they would be able to do more than that.

23. COBWEBS

Anna gave everyone a lift home after dinner. Daisy waved goodbye to her friends and felt a mixture of emotions. She loved her family so much that she would do anything for them, but there was a part of her that really didn't want to go into the cottage. Scott's house had been warm with laughter, good-natured teasing, and life. She'd sat opposite Liam at dinner. At first she could feel waves of guilt coming off him. She'd done her best to give him the impression that she held no hard feelings towards him, because after all he had stood between her and Dillon. She also didn't want Scott to be angry with Liam for too long. Scott loved his brother dearly and it was painful to be angry at someone you care so much about. She was glad Liam's guilt lessened over dinner. Other people's guilt could really sap the appetite. Dinner had been a noisy affair full of laughter.

Daisy took a deep breath and let it out slowly. It was

hard to laugh in a place where someone was dying. She knew that Granddad wasn't in any pain and was comfortable; when he did pass-over he would be with her Mum and Dad, but she wouldn't see him anymore; it was always hard to say goodbye to someone you love – and she'd had to do that far to often for a child of her years. Nan didn't want him to leave, and there was something going on between Nan and Uncle Allen that made Daisy feel uncomfortable. She didn't exactly know what was going on but it was oppressive.

Then there was Uncle Jack, trying his best to be calm, but she could feel his tension pulled so tight that there was a danger of it snapping. Uncle Allen had asked Dr. Zhi to come over. She had worked with Uncle Allen on a lot of cases including when they had found Uncle Jack. Uncle Jack liked her. Dr Zhi's was also a Doctor of Psychology and she knew how to heal people. It was thanks to her that Jack had gone to university to study medicine.

Even now, Jack saw her as a mentor.

When Daisy opened the front door she was met by the strong smell of tea-tree oil, which meant someone had been doing the housework. She kicked off her shoes and put them in the cupboard under the stairs in case Albie took a fancy to one of them. The carpet felt slightly damp through her socks, which told her that someone had also washed it.

Anna had given Megan and Daisy a plastic shopping bag full of homemade pastries that gave off a lovely smell every time the bag moved. Daisy took them into the kitchen so her family could help themselves. She found Una sitting at the kitchen table her hands wrapped round a large mug of tea. Sat opposite her was Jack with his head resting on the table. He was wearing blue and white pyjamas, which looked as though they'd been used to clean the kitchen floor.

Una looked at her and gave her a smile. "Hello love," she said. "Did you have a nice time at Scott's?"

"It was lovely thanks," Daisy replied. She held up the bag. "Scott's Mum gave us some pastries." She put them down on the work surface. "What about you? Are you okay?"

"Well I've calmed down now as you can probably sense," Una said. "I don't like it when you're hurt." She held out her hand towards Daisy. "How's the eye feeling?"

Daisy took her hand. "It's a bit sore but it's alright."

"Come and sit on my lap," Una said quietly.

"Nan?" Daisy was surprised at the sudden request. "I might squash you."

"I don't care," Una said. "Come on, give me a hug."

Carefully, Daisy sat down on Una's lap. She wrapped her arms around Daisy. She breathed in Daisy's flowery shampoo and thought about how she missed the little girl Daisy used to be. She had been so happy, always giggling; playing in the woods and coming back covered in dirt and leaves. She loved the young woman Daisy was becoming, she laughed but she no longer giggled – which was a pity. She would sit quietly in the woods for hours on end, thinking thoughts too heavy for a child. She was studious and seemed convinced that it was her duty to take care of everything and everyone. She'd become so serious. Una missed that giggle.

"Sweetheart is something bothering you?" Una asked.

"Megan met a ghost of a little girl who drowned in the hotel garden," Daisy said quietly.

"Poor little mite," Una replied.

Daisy nodded. "She won't pass over because her Mum told her that if she ever got lost she should stay right where she was and her Mum would come and find her."

"I remember telling you the same thing," Una nodded. "Her Mum must be still alive if she's still there, otherwise she would have come for her by now."

"That's what we think," Daisy replied. "We tried to look up her death on the Internet but there wasn't anything, which seemed strange. I would have thought that would have been big news at the time. We want to look her up in the newspapers at the library but we haven't got an idea what year she died." She looked at Jack. "I thought maybe Uncle Jack could do a psychometric reading for us, but I didn't realise how poorly he was. How sick is he?"

"He's only got a broken ankle," Una said, gently brushing Daisy's hair with her fingers. "He's not sick."

"Then why is he wearing pajamas this time of day?" Daisy asked. "And why does he look like he's used them to do the housework?"

Una sighed. She hadn't kept Patrick's dementia a secret from Daisy because she would have soon noticed that her granddad getting more forgetful and confused, and she had refused to tell her that Patrick was going to get better after the stroke, because he wasn't and sometimes protecting a child through lies is just a delayed cruelty. However, as much as Una wanted to talk to Daisy about Jack, she just couldn't bring herself to. Patrick's illness could be safely linked to age – something the young don't have to worry about, but when an illness of the mind attacked somebody young, how could that be explained?

"Apart from the bedrooms, he's cleaned the house from top to bottom," Una replied. "At some point, and I don't know how he did it he managed it, he got into the wall space to ask a mouse not to chew the wiring because it was making a mess. He's bored and it's making him ill. Clearly rest and recuperation isn't what the doctor should be ordering."

Daisy slid off her Nan's lap and opened the kitchen cupboards one after one. Every tin and packet had been put in alphabetical order.

"Don't try and protect me, Nan, because that means you're going to lie to me and I don't want that," Daisy said quietly. She looked back at the cupboards, "I don't understand this, it's like he's trying to keep everything in order."

Una took a deep breath. "You remember what I told you about Uncle Jack's Mum?" Daisy nodded. "When Uncle Jack wouldn't use his abilities to blackmail people, she sold him to some people, some bad people, who did some very evil things; things I don't ever want to, tell you about. That's when Uncle Allen found him."

Daisy of course knew that Uncle Allen had found Jack, but she hadn't been told where and how. As much as Daisy wanted to hear Jack's story, part of her really didn't want to. Once she knew, there would be no taking it back. Una continued, "Sometimes when something very bad has happened to someone, their mind gets broken. It doesn't always happen instantly, it can be like hairline cracks in a plate; over the years those cracks make the plate weaker and the plate finally cracks. You can stick it back together, but there will always be a weakness there – always a danger of it cracking again. That's why he's in his pajamas. He was threatening to go to work, so I hid his clothes. It was a mistake." She gestured to the kitchen cupboards.

"Maybe getting him out of the house would be a good thing?" Daisy said.

Una nodded. "Certainly keeping him cooped up isn't working. I'll talk with Uncle Allen and see what he thinks. Why don't you go and have a bath and get into your pajamas. We'll have some of those pastries Scott's Mum made for supper."

Daisy left the kitchen but not before she looked back at Jack. Una could tell by her granddaughter's eyes that she was trying very hard not to cry.

Allen came home long after Daisy had gone to bed. He had moved back into Cobwebs to help Una look after Patrick, and to help Jack for as long as his ankle took to heal. Jack had woken up from a nightmare and stiffly hobbled off to his room, although Una knew that it wasn't to rest.

"How was your day?" Una asked, serving her son a large bowl of homemade soup.

"Finished the case," Allen answered sitting down. "Not that you're really interested, are you? I can tell by the look in your eyes that something has happened." He looked at the clock on the kitchen wall. "And you're usually in bed by now and my dinner left in the microwave."

Una sat down opposite him and smiled. "Ever the detective." She smoothed her skirt over her knees. "Jack didn't have a good day. I hid his clothes to stop him going to work, and he became... anxious."

"Probably because he felt confined," Allen replied. "So that explains why the place looks like it's been cleaned by a hyperactive maid with obsessive compulsive disorder."

"He probably wouldn't have been so bad if Daisy hadn't gotten hurt today," Una said.

Allen looked at her. "What?"

"Some boys wanted to see her cry, and when she stood up for herself; they didn't like it. One of them punched her. She has a black eye... she didn't retaliate."

"I'm glad to hear it."

"She still went to her friend's house after school."

Allen raised an eyebrow, a habit he had when wanting more information.

"Scott Brown. You met his granddad once, remember? Reg Brown kept snooping around that malicious haunting you were investigating?"

Allen nodded recalling the man and the incident.

"Megan was there and she told them how there's a ghost of a little girl haunting the hotel garden."

"Where is this going, Mum?"

"They don't know when the little girl died. She won't move on because she was told by her Mum that if she was ever lost she should stay exactly where she is, so they've guess her Mum is still alive. Daisy thought Jack could do a psychometric reading to find out the year, but she came home and saw... well she saw what you have, only with Jack passed out at the table, and she didn't think it was a good idea."

"And you think it is?" Allen asked.

The sound of crutches stopped Una's response. Jack hobbled into the kitchen. The sleep he'd had earlier hadn't done him any good, in fact to Una he looked more tired and pale. He had changed out of his dusty pajamas into a clean pair and had washed his hands and face, and brushed his hair.

"I think you need to stop talking about me as though I'm not able to make a decision for myself," he said tensely. "There's a child out there who's waiting for a mother who probably won't be coming to get her for years, and there are three children willing to help her. I don't think we should discourage them by not assisting them in whatever way possible."

Una swore under her breath. Even when there wasn't a full moon, Jack had exceptional hearing.

"Jack, sweetheart... " she said gently.

"My mind is like a cracked plate?" Jack asked leaning against the doorframe. Una felt uneasy she had honestly thought Jack had been asleep when she had told Daisy that, "Thank you! I really wanted Daisy to think I'm about to break at any moment; one more person she feels responsible for!"

"You were asleep at the kitchen table," Allen said softly. "I'm sure Daisy guessed you weren't right before Una spoke with her; it was pretty obvious. Come and sit down, please."

Jack sat down at the kitchen table and the effort seemed to exhaust him.

"There are times when you're not yourself," Allen said. Jack opened his mouth to say something witty about being werewolf but was cut off by Allen's hand. "No! Just listen for a moment. You've been through a lot and it's amazing that you're not in a hospital – possibly in a padded room somewhere. You've done more than well with your job and helping Mum with Dad and Daisy, but, and I know you don't like to admit it to yourself, sometimes you're the one to be looked after. Sometimes you're the one who people must take responsibility for, because you are liable to push yourself so hard to your limits that you will break, and you will end up in that hospital." Jack's jaw clenched tightly and he balled his hands up into tight fists. He knew it was pointless trying to argue otherwise. Allen was right, but that didn't make it easier to swallow. "We don't want that, Jack, so there will be times when we need to talk about things. There will be times when we make decisions that are right for the greater good. Do you understand what I'm saying?"

"Personal welfare is of no concern whilst others are suffering," Jack chanted refusing to look at Allen's eyes.

Allen moved closer and placed his hands over Jack's fists, "Jack, how do you think Daisy would feel if you put your personal welfare at risk for something she'd asked you to do?"

Jack didn't have to think very hard to know the answer to that; she'd always blame herself.

"What do we do?" he asked quietly.

"We'll have something to eat and drink," Allen replied, "and then we'll talk."

24. THE READING

Roy Brown sat in his car looking at the hotel. When Liam had told him the story about the little ghost girl Megan had seen and wanted to help pass over, he had decided to do a little Stone Towers research of his own. He'd discovered that it used to be called Calculus Castle, and was built in 1420 for the Stone family. During the 1900s, when the building was going under some much-needed repair, the skeleton of a baby was found under the kitchen floor. It helped cement Stone Tower's haunted reputation. Many people had reported the feeling of being watched, of dark shadows walking the corridors and disappearing into walls. Some of the funnier haunting stories had been of women having their bottoms pinched, and many men who had slept in room 1348 reported having been pulled out of bed by their hair. But not one of the haunting stories mentioned a little girl in the garden. In the passenger seat next to him, Scott shivered.

"Are you alright, mate?" he asked. "Do you need me to put the heating on?"

Scott shook his head and rubbed his hands together. "I don't want to get too warm otherwise I'll freeze when were out in the garden."

"Good point." Roy nodded looking up at the rain-filled clouds. "So, what did Daisy tell you about her uncle?"

"He's a Psyche. He can do Psychometry and he's a forensic pathologist." Scott told him "Granddad, did Mum talk to you before we left?"

Roy looked away from the clouds back to Scott. Anne had reminded him that this was purely about helping a little girl cross over, not the beginning of an adventure to satisfy Roy's curiosity for all things supernatural and paranormal.

"Yes," Roy said. "I didn't ask your friends too many questions when they came over the other day, did I?"

"No, but then Mum was there and she would have told you off," Scott replied. "Like she did when you interviewed Daisy's Nan at the school gates that time, remember?"

"I wasn't interviewing her," Roy protested. "I was just interested. Your Mum would have never have known if you and Liam hadn't told her."

"Yes she would; Mum always finds out things in the end."

"Yes," Roy said softly. "Creepy, isn't it?"

"Yeah," Scott said sounding thoughtful. A movement outside took his attention. "They're here."

Roy looked and did his very best to suppress a groan.

Allen Monroe had been told that Roy was coming and to say that he wasn't happy about it would have been a serious understatement. Years ago, Allen was investigating a particularly nasty haunting in a small bed and breakfast somewhere in Wiltshire. It had got so bad that the owners had to cancel bookings for safety reasons. Roy had come along as a paranormal investigator; his investigations not only distressed the family involved but he had wound up the entity so much that it nearly dragged everything and one into the dark dimension. Allen had reported Roy to the authorities to ensure that he couldn't come anywhere near another investigation. He had thought (hoped) that would be the last time he would see the irritating Bland.

"What's wrong, Uncle Allen?" Daisy asked quietly.

"I know Scott's grandfather," Allen replied. "He nearly destroyed an investigation I was on."

"Oh!"

"It's nothing you should feel responsible for," Allen said, placing his hand on her shoulder. "You go along with Scott and let Megan know we're here."

Allen got the wheelchair he had hired for Jack out of the boot. Jack had said he would be more than capable of using his crutches, but Allen had said chair or home. Jack was happy to endure anything to get out of Cobwebs.

"So when you said he nearly destroyed the investigation you were on...?" Jack inquired politely as he maneuvered himself into the chair.

"His antics nearly pulled me and Lily-Anne into a completely different dimension which many would call Hell." Allen clicked the chairs footplates into place irritably.

"Right so any annoyance towards him today will be entirely understandable," Jack gave with a small nod.

"What's wrong with your Uncle Allen?" Scott asked as they walked to Megan's front door. "He looks stressed."

"He doesn't really like your granddad," Daisy replied bluntly. "He interfered with an investigation Uncle Allen was conducting."

"He's a paranormal investigator too?" Scott asked.

"Sort of." Daisy smiled wryly.

"Well," Scott said feeling as though he should stand up for his granddad, "how do we know that it wasn't your uncle who interfered with granddad's investigation?"

"Uncle Allen is employed by the government; if he's been called in then it means something could be life threatening," Daisy replied. "Your granddad hasn't had any training has he? And at a guess he didn't start being a paranormal investigator until he retired?"

"Okay," Scott held his hands up in mock submission, "you win."

Daisy frowned, "I didn't know that we were having a competition."

Megan came to the front door smiling. When she saw that they were giving each other dark looks, frowned.

"Is something wrong?" she asked.

"Daisy brought her other uncle with her," Scott told her. "He knows my Granddad and he doesn't like him." Scott couldn't hide the hurt in his voice.

"Your Uncle Allen?" Megan replied. "He's here?"

"Uncle Jack has been feeling tired because of his ankle," Daisy felt annoyed at Scott for telling Megan about Uncle Allen not liking Scott's Granddad; it wasn't likely to get in the way of helping India so why make Megan worry. "Uncle Allen is here to help him after he's done the reading." She looked at Scott. "It won't stop us from helping India so don't worry."

"Are you two okay?" Megan asked.

"Of course," Daisy answered. "What goes on between Uncle Allen and Roy has nothing to do with Scott and me."

"Right." Scott nodded, glad when he saw Daisy smile at him.

It was decided that Jack would do the psychometric reading before they went into the hotel for tea so that they'd have time to discuss it in style afterwards.

Tabitha had joined the party and was doing her best to look important. "He looks like he needs more than a cup of tea and some posh cake and sandwiches to make him feel better," Tabitha said pouting in the direction of Jack. Megan had the instant impression that Tabitha found him attractive. "A big bowl of chicken soup and a few days in bed with me is what I'd prescribe."

"Tabitha!" Megan gasped. The group looked around and Megan found herself having to make a sudden excuse. "Could you not suddenly appear like that, you made me jump."

"Megan, please remind Tabitha that I'm also able to see and *hear* her!" Jack called back from his wheelchair, "I don't eat chicken soup. I'm a vegetarian."

If spirit guides could blush, Tabitha would have done.

"A vegetarian werewolf, well that's different," she said

taking a drag on her cigarette.

"You've got The Glow too?" Scott asked.

"I've got a chemical imbalance in my brain that makes it possible for me to see ghosts and spirits," Jack answered.

"Is it serious?" Scott asked worried.

"No not serious at all," Jack replied before whispering something to Allen.

"I take it that Scott doesn't know that Jack is a werewolf?" Tabitha asked Megan. She shook her head. "Well it's probably for the best."

"Why are you here?" Megan whispered.

"There are ghosts in that building," Tabitha replied. "Ghosts that don't want to cross over; they're happy where they are, they might think with your Glow that you're here to exorcize them and they may get nasty about it."

"How do you know that they're nasty?" Megan whispered.

"I didn't say that they are nasty, I'm saying that they may *get* nasty." Tabitha lit another cigarette and Megan gave her a disapproving look.

"I know you're already dead, but that whole smoking thing is still disgusting!" Megan said

"What can I say some habits don't die with you," Tabitha shrugged , "I'm going to hang around to make sure that you're safe."

"What could they do to me if you weren't here?" Megan whispered.

"I'm not going anywhere, so you don't have to worry!" Tabitha punctuated her sentence with a victorious smile.

It didn't stop Megan worrying.

They went to India's pond, careful to approach as casually as possible so that it wouldn't frighten her.

Allen assisted Jack from the wheelchair and helped him to get his balance. He looked at Jack steadily. "Remember," he said quietly, "any sign of trouble and I'm stopping you whatever way possible. The child's mother will come for her eventually, your health is the most important priority here."

Jack sighed and Allen tightened his grip around his arms. "I'll be fine. I do this as my living. I know when to stop."

Jack sat with his legs stretched out in front of him and his hands resting on his knees. He always prepared himself in this way before a reading. You never knew exactly what you were going to experience, especially with the land so full of history. Jack could hear birds singing and something living scuttling in the leaves under the bushes; animals could sense evil and unless they had loyalty to a human they stayed as far away from it as possible. The fact that animals were still around was reassuring. An icy wind blew, carrying the sound of sobbing across the water's edge. The child needed help; she was suffering. Taking a deep breath, Jack placed his hands on the ground, closed his eyes and opened up his mind.

Megan jumped as Jack took in a short sharp breath and then held it. His eyes moved under the eyelids as though he was in a deep sleep and he was dreaming. His mouth moved as though he was talking to someone or something, but no words were coming out.

"How long do we leave him like this?" she asked quietly.

"He knows when to stop, don't worry," Allen replied not taking his eyes off Jack.

Jack's body began to tremble and grew pale. His lips took on a pale blue colour. Daisy felt her hands warming with healing energy and took several steps towards him, only to have Allen put his hand up to stop her.

"I know you want to help but any sudden change might send him into shock," he said softly.

Scott slipped his hand into Daisy's, which seemed to take him as much by surprise as Daisy. But she didn't flinch away, instead she curled her fingers around Scott's warm skin. Allen glanced down and felt a pang of guilt at being irritated with the boy's questions earlier. Jack suddenly yanked his hands off the ground, capturing everybody's attention. His eyes flew open but he wasn't looking at anyone. His head was thrown back and he was coughing large grey clouds that evaporated just seconds they came into the light. This happened three or four time before he collapsed onto his back, breathing heavily.

"Jack?" Allen crouched down. "Can you hear me? Do you know where you are?"

"Someone stole my warmth," Jack murmured.

"I think we should get you inside for a cup of tea," Allen said.

"I like it here," Jack said drowsily. He pointed lazily at the sky. "That cloud looks like a bunny rabbit."

"Is he alright?" Megan asked as Allen helped a floppy Jack into a sitting position.

"This happens sometimes when he's done a psychometric reading," Daisy said. "I don't really understand it, it's something to do with the brain and having all of it working at the same time, but on different levels. It takes a while for certain parts to shut down. It leaves him a little bit loopy for a bit."

"And no one notices it when this happens where he

works?" Scott asked.

"They know what he can do at work," Daisy replied. "You can't use abilities like Psychometry without someone eventually noticing – especially when you're working for the police. They usually give him a cup of tea, a few biscuits and make him lie down for a little while."

"Have I had seizure?" Jack asked. "I don't feel like I've had a seizure… my bum is really cold."

"That's because you're sitting down on the cold ground," Allen said patiently.

"I can't feel it," Jack frowned. "It's really peculiar. Is it still there?"

"Would you like some help?" Roy offered, taking a small step forward. "The couple over there are beginning to stare."

Allen glanced over his shoulder and noticed a man and woman who were huddled together. He looked back at Roy and nodded. "Thank you."

Taking an arm each Allen and Roy helped Jack to his feet and sat him down in the wheelchair. Allen then pushed Jack towards the hotel with the others closely following.

25. AFTERNOON TEA.

The tearoom of the hotel was busy. There was the constant buzz of people having conversations, china clinking against china, and cutlery tapping plates. They sat down, taking the table tucked away in one of the large bay windows. Plates of cream cakes and small cucumber sandwiches with their crusts cut off arrived. The children, and Jack, were given large china cups with hot chocolate and whipped cream, whilst Roy and Allen helped themselves to the teapot.

"What I'd like to know is what your plans are if you are able to find the girl's parents." Allen said.

"I'm... I'm really not sure," Megan answered. "I talked to Mr Gibbs to help his wife cross-over so I guess I could do the same thing."

Allen shook his head. "This situation is different. You know Mr Gibbs and were able to go up to him after school," he replied. "I don't like the idea of you going to a stranger's house on your own."

"Scott and I could go with her," Daisy said.

Scott had his mouth full of cream cake but nodded enthusiastically.

"These people have lost a child," Allen said. "Three children turning up and telling them that they've seen that child's ghost... well we don't know how they'd react."

"I could go with them," Roy offered.

"And they would assume that you were using them in some money-making scheme," Allen replied. "Especially if you attempt to help them in explaining how ghosts are possible." He took a sip of tea. "I've had to sit through that before," he muttered under his breath.

"I've learnt a lot since then," Roy said gripping his teacup tightly to try and contain his humiliation.

"I think you need..." Allen began putting a scone on Jack's plate. Megan stopped listening to Allen as she was distracted by a Spider Monkey in a red coat that jumped onto the table and sat between the cake plates. Only Jack and Megan seemed to notice its presence. The others continued forking cake into their mouths completely oblivious. Jack leaned in and whispered, "Please tell me that you can see it too?"

"Yep," Megan said, still not quite believing her eyes.

"Tabitha?" she asked shakily, "Why is there a monkey on the table?"

The whole party turned and looked at Megan as if she were crazy, and then to Jack who simply nodded his head as if to suggest that if Megan were crazy then he was too.

"Is it a residual?"

"Residuals don't look at you," informed Tabitha. "This little fella probably died in the eighteenth century by the look of the outfit he's wearing."

"How do you get animal ghosts to pass over?" Megan asked as the monkey groomed its tail.

Tabitha carefully picked the monkey up and it gave a small noise of surprise; it had been a long time since it had felt a human touch. It looked at its new mistress and scrambled up onto her shoulder, wrapping its tail around her neck.

"I'll see if he comes with me when I leave," Tabitha said gently, tickling the monkey under its chin. "That's if he wants too, he may want to stay here."

"Could you take India with you?" Megan asked hopefully. "You could tell her that you're going to take her to her Mummy and then… you know?"

"It doesn't work like that." Tabitha sighed. "She wants her Mummy and that's her unfinished business. She can't pass over until she's finished; that's the rules."

"What did Tabitha say?" Scott asked when Megan told him he frowned "Who made these rules? Ask her why she can't just ask them to change them."

"You don't talk to them," Tabitha said, lighting a cigarette. "They talk to you."

Jack suddenly became animated. "I've learnt in the past that it's in the interest of everyone's to follow the rules of 'They'."

Allen looked at his watch and recovered a pill pot from his pocket, placing three coloured pills onto Jack's saucer. Jack looked hacked off about the gesture. "I really don't want to take these here, I've only just got my head back together!"

"Do I need to remind you of our agreement?" Allen whispered with gritted teeth. Jack threw the pills into his mouth and took a mouthful of chocolate, swallowing them down with a grimace. Everybody else did their best to find something out of the window to look at whilst Allen and Jack fought it out. Jack opened his mouth wide and waggled his tongue; Allen didn't look amused.

"Do you have any idea when India died?" he asked.

"By the fashion, early nineties," Jack replied.

Allen stopped glaring at Jack and turned his attention

back to the rest of the group. "If it's okay with Megan's parents, I'll take her and Daisy back home to Cobwebs and we'll discuss how India's parents are going to be approached." He looked at Roy. "If you and Scott could perhaps go to the library and find anything in the archives and then meet us there?"

Roy and Scott nodded in unison, glad to be involved.

Allen then addressed Megan, "If Tabitha is joining us please ask her to make sure she leaves the monkey behind, we've got enough on with my Dad's dog haunting the cottage at the moment – it would be a total circus if we throw a monkey into the room too."

Looking back to Tabitha and the ridiculous monkey, a thought hit her. "Ghosts can touch spirits!" she said.

"Well yes, of course." Tabitha nodded, puzzled that Megan had stated the obvious.

Megan found herself breaking into a smile. She'd just had the perfect idea on how to convince India that she was a ghost.

26. COMFORT

Brenda Monroe stormed into Cobwebs, her long, blond hair flowing behind her. 'A break!' she recalled John's hurtful words. She couldn't believe that after all the long talks they had about telling their family that they were going to become an item, he'd decided that it would be a good idea to have a 'break' from one another to spend time with other people; just so they knew for certain that this was what they both wanted. There had to be someone else, she thought, and he hadn't had the guts to tell her. Well if he thought she was going to…

"Brenda?" Allen came down the stairs, "What's wrong?"

She was about to tell him; whine to her big brother about how unfair their cousin was being, and then she remembered what he was doing back at the cottage after he'd moved out three years ago. It meant Jack had arrived. The planning had taken months to prepare, and Brenda at first wondered why a twenty year old would need adopting (after all he was only two years younger than her) and then Allen had told them the story of The Place, and showed her the pictures, or at least the pictures he was allowed to show them. All had become clear. Her anger and resentment was replaced by curiosity.

"May I go and see him?" she asked.

Allen nodded. "Just for a few seconds," he said. "It's going to take him a while to get used to the idea that he's safe and has a home with a family."

Jack lay on his new bed and looked at the patterns on the ceiling. The medicine Dr Zhi had given him made him sleepy and he found he could only concentrate on things for a short time, but she told him that he wouldn't be on them for very long; it was just until he got used to being away from the shelter of the hospital he had been staying in. He heard movement downstairs but it seemed to be very far away. Allen came back in and placed his hand gently onto his arm.

"Jack," he said softly, "Brenda is here to say hello to you."

Jack sat up slowly and looked at the young woman coming into the room smiling at him, she looked like a much younger version of Una.

"Hello," he said, his voice slightly slurred from the medication he was on.

Brenda had been warned that for the first few days Jack would be groggy. Allen had arranged for people to come to the cottage to help him adjust to the outside world. Slowly the medicine would be reduced.

"Hello Jack," she said gently. "You're really sleepy aren't you? Would you like to lie back down?"

Jack nodded. He could hear Brenda and Allen talking (probably about him) but he didn't really care, not right then, all he wanted to do was sleep.

Unfortunately sleep came with nightmares, and he woke up panicking and fighting with the sheets, until a warm comforting presence cut through the fear. He opened his eyes in the dimly lit room and found himself looking at Brenda.

"I'm sorry," he whispered, thinking he must have woken her. He was surprised he hadn't woken everyone in the building.

"It's okay, sweetheart," she soothed as she gently stroked his hair. "You poor thing, you're shaking – come here."

Carefully she helped Jack sit up and pulled him into a hug, gently rubbing his back, sad at how long it took for him to relax. At first, he was reluctant to wrap his arms around her and she wondered how long it been since he had felt loved. As soon as the question came to mind, a thought came to her; John wanted them to have a break and spend time with different people, well Jack was certainly different, she decided. She gently kissed him on the cheek, slowly moving to his lips.

Jack was gently shaken awake and when he opened his eyes, he found himself in the front seat of Allen's car. His head felt fuzzy, and for a few minutes he wasn't entirely sure how he got there.

"Jack," Allen said gently, "we're home." Jack blinked at him. "Are you alright?"

"Everything is all cloudy but yet I can see," Jack mumbled.

Allen looked at him sympathetically. "It's the pills, remember? You need a little rest from your ability; it's only for a little while, I promise."

"I had a dream... I think... no memory... maybe a little bit of both." Jack frowned. "It's fading... gone."

"Well if it was important I'm sure you'll remember it later," Allen said gently. "Come on, I'll help you."

Jack nodded and touched his lips wondering why they were tingling.

27. THE PLAN

Even though Daisy had warned Megan about Albi, she still let out a little squeak when she took off her shoes and one disappeared right in front of her, only to materialise a few seconds later in the mouth of a ghost-dog, whose tail was wagging madly with excitement. Instinctively, Megan held out her hand to let him sniff it, but Albi had other ideas; he was already dashing down the hallway wanting to play chase.

"It's okay, I'll get it," Tabitha said, running after him. Her giggles floated through the house. It was the first time Megan had seen Tabitha anywhere near happy.

"So how can some ghosts touch things and others can't?" Megan asked.

"Ghosts can't touch things," Daisy replied, putting her shoes into the cupboard. "Spirits can. Everything gives off an energy whether they're alive or not, and they use this to pick things up and move them, it's like rubbing a balloon against your hair and then using the static electricity to pick up bits of paper, only it's much more complicated than that. Ghosts can't pick things up because their energy is weaker. When they cross-over they get a kind of power boost."

"And ghosts and spirits can touch each other?" Megan asked following Daisy into the living room.

"They're both made of the same energy it's like me being able to touch you."

Daisy stopped to watch Allen help Jack into one of the living room chairs. She'd never seen Jack so weak but he seemed to have woken up a bit.

Tabitha returned from her game of chase with Albi. She was surprisingly breathless with play. "I left your shoe in the cupboard along with the others."

"Thanks. By the way, I think I've got an idea that could show India that she's a ghost," Megan announced. Everyone stopped to look at her. "Okay, here's my plan. I'm not sure it's going to definitely work but it might. Tabitha, you could say that you will wait with India so that she won't be lonely – you could tell her your name and shake her hand and then ask her if she would like to throw some stones into the pond to pass the time. I used to like to do that when I was little. Then when she tried to pick up the stones, she'll discover that she can't..." Revealing her plan out aloud made her realise how flawed it was. "Would that be really cruel?"

Jack was the first to speak. "It'll probably scare her. If you think about it, no one would really want to hear that they're dead but she needs to know and there isn't any easy way to tell her. What you've got in mind sounds like the gentlest way of going about it."

"And when she realises she's a ghost, she'll be able to move away from the pond?" Megan asked.

"Well from what you've said, the only thing that's keeping India here is India." Tabitha offered. "I can keep her company until we decide how to break the news to her parents."

"That's if we can find her parents."

"We're about to find out," Jack said. "I've just heard Roy's car pull up outside." Three knocks came from the front door. "And there they are."

Scott came into the living room clutching a piece of paper, with Roy following close by.

"We found out about India in the Gloaming News," Scott announced, proudly passing the piece of paper to Megan.

"Brilliant! That's great news."

Scott had photocopied a page from the newspaper. The

title read simply, 'Girl, 6, Drowns in Hotel Pond'. Megan looked at the date at the top of the paper. Jack had been right; India had died in the early nineties.

"What does it say?" Daisy asked.

Megan scanned over the page and read out the opening, "A six-year-old girl was found yesterday drowned in the ornamental pond at Stone Towers hotel. Situated five miles from the popular tourist town of Threshold, the hotel is a well-known landmark. It is believed that her devastated parents thought she was playing safely with her fifteen year old brother." Megan swallowed hard at the sight of the picture of India. She was holding a white rabbit and grinning into the lens of the camera; she looked so full of life. Who could have known when that photo was taken, how short her life would be?

"India was found twenty minutes after her distraught mother and father noticed she was missing. It is thought that she strayed away from her brother, when he became distracted." Megan looked up at the group who were listening to her intently. "India said he was talking to some boys."

"He must feel awful," Roy said sympathetically. "What else does it say?"

"She had been playing with a ball when last seen and

its believed she dropped it into the pond. She fell in trying to get it." Megan carried on reading, "Her brother Luke tried to revive her but was unsuccessful. India was taken to hospital, where it she was later pronounced that she had died. Police are treating it as a tragic accident. Her parents Hilary, 40 and Richard 45 (both lawyers), released a statement yesterday, 'There are no words to express how we are feeling right now; we can't believe that our beautiful little girl was so tragically taken away from us. We would do anything to hear, see and hold her again.' The couple who live in Gloaming, Surrey, say they will be forever grateful for those who tried to save their little girl and would like to thank everyone for their efforts." Megan looked up. "Where is Gloaming?"

"It's about eight miles from here," Roy answered. "Lovely place."

"So what do we do? Look up Richard and Hilary Cole in the phone book?" Megan asked.

"I could help you with finding her parents," Allen said. "You just concentrate on getting India into believing that she's a ghost."

"Could you find her sister first?" Megan asked. "She was the one who taught India about ghosts and spirits; the sister will probably believe us and then she can help us to convince her parents."

"That's if her beliefs haven't changed," Allen said. "Remember, she'll be an adult now and beliefs change, especially after suffering tragedy."

Megan's shoulders dropped.

Daisy placed her hand over Megan's and gave it a reassuring squeeze. "Uncle Allen isn't saying we shouldn't try her first, are you?"

"No, not at all. I'm trying to prepare you that everything may not go smoothly."

Megan nodded. Tabitha had already warned her that they might not be able to help India to crossover, but with everything they'd found out so far, Megan was beginning to feel hopeful that they would be able to succeed.

28. HELLO INDIA.

India Cole stood by the pond and wondered why her Mummy hadn't come. She felt like she had been waiting for days and days, which she was sure wasn't true because Mummy wouldn't have left her for that long, nor would Zoe or Luke, and even Daddy would have come and found her by now. India looked around her, she'd been crying and no one had come to ask her what was wrong. Well apart from that ghost – she had talked to her. She had looked like a nice ghost; not scary at all.

"Hello," a voice said. "Are you alright? Have you hurt yourself?"

India looked up at to see a lady standing nearby. No, not a lady, she looked the same age as Zoe perhaps, and people called her a girl.

"Oh sweetie," she walked over to her and crouched down. She wiped her cheeks with her fingers. "Tell me what happened, I might be able to help."

"I can't find my Mummy," India sobbed.

"You must be feeling really lonely," the girl said kindly. "Would you like me to wait with you until your Mummy comes?"

"I'm really not allowed to talk to strangers," India replied.

"Well, we don't have to talk. We can throw stones and see who can make the biggest splash. I always find that if I do something then time always goes quicker."

She threw the stone into the water where it made a small splash, "Hmm, that wasn't very good was it?"

India smiled and shook her head. She looked around and saw a big stone poking out of the dirt. She bent down and picked it up, only her fingers went through it just as though it were air. India frowned thinking she must be imagining things. Daddy always said a person's imagination could make them think silly things. She would try another stone but the same thing happened again and again.

No, she shook her head: this wasn't right. She reached for a stick and her fingers went through that as well.

"What's going on?" she wailed. "Why can't I pick anything up?"

She stared at the girl. She had a strange expression on her face. She looked very sad. India looked around the garden. Summer had gone. The leaves had left the trees. India knew it was winter, but she wasn't feeling cold, she was wearing her summer dress but she wasn't shivering.

"I want to go home," India said. "Please, I want my Mummy and I want to go home."

"I need you to listen to me," the girl told her gently. "My name is Tabitha, and I've been sent here by a very good friend to help you and explain a few things."

29. HALF-TERM

When she had lived back in London, Megan had spent the half-term break doing her homework and going to the shops with the occasional trip to The Natural History Museum or The Tate Gallery, and going round Sarah's house. (Sarah and her hadn't talked for some time now, Megan had been too busy with her life at Threshold and Sarah was often out with Sophie when she called anyway.)

She never imagined that she would one day be waiting for her spirit guide to come and meet her to help them with a ghost-child who'd been stuck in a hotel garden for years. Megan managed to do most of her holiday homework and Cheryl agreed that it was okay for Megan to go and meet Scott and Daisy in town. She might not have been so agreeable if she'd known what they were really up to.

Allen had found out that Zoe was working in one of the teashops in town, and they were able to go there to get lunch. Megan really hoped Tabitha would be able to convince India to come with them.

A smell of cigarette smoke wafted in behind her. She turned to see Tabitha holding India's hand.

"Hello, Tabitha. Hello, India."

India stared at her feet. "I'm sorry I shouted at you," she whispered.

"It's alright. If I saw someone glowing then I'd think they were a ghost too."

India nodded and then her bottom lip began to wobble.

"Oh sweetheart!" Tabitha put her arms around her. "It's going to be alright. Remember what we talked about?"

"No it's not," India sobbed. "I'm a ghost. I can't give my Mummy or Daddy a cuddle, and you said they might not even be able to see me." She pushed Tabitha away. "Why can't we find my body so I can get back in it; then I won't be dead – then everything would be alright!"

"Please believe us, India, if it could be done... but it can't," Tabitha said gently.

"When you find Mummy and Daddy," India said quietly "can I..." she swallowed, "can I stay with them?"

Megan knew the answer but she didn't know how to put it into words that wouldn't hurt the child even more.

"You could," Tabitha said, "but would you really want to stay where no one can see or hear you?"

India shook her head.

"You really need to go to Heaven but before you go it will be nice to say goodbye to your family. And remember, these kind of goodbyes aren't forever – one day your Mummy and Daddy will be with you."

"How are we going to find them?" she asked.

"I've some really good friends who are helping me and one of them has found your sister." Megan told her.

"Really?" India broke into a big smile and clapped her hands.

"She's a lot older than you remember," Megan said. "When you're a ghost..."

"I know, time goes really slowly and when you're alive time goes really quickly. Tabitha told me. But she's still my sister."

"Yes," Megan agreed, "she's still your sister. There's something I also need you to tell you about my friend Daisy... She looks a bit different to other girls."

30. ZOE

If Zoe Cole put her mind to it she'd have made a wonderful Marilyn Monroe lookalike, and her friend, Louise, continually reminded her how much money she could make if only she would put on a bit more weight and bleach her hair. Zoe had said she would rather look like the Norma-Jean Baker that Marilyn had been before Hollywood had got their hands on her. At the end of the day, Zoe just wanted to be herself. She enjoyed working in Hatter's Teashop five days a week and chatting to the customers – even if she did have to wear a ridiculous dress modelled on Louis Carroll's, Alice. Zoe liked being a friendly ear to those who wanted someone to listen to their problems or share their news. She enjoyed listening to the older customers' stories. Every Thursday, Friday and Saturday night she sang Rhythm and Blues, and sometimes Jazz, at Nightingale's Night Club. She enjoyed the glamour of those nights and the way that people danced to her singing, but she knew if she did it every night it would definitely loose its sparkle. Her Dad wasn't pleased with her decision; she was thirty-three years old, he reminded her; she should be thinking of a serious career. He had spent a fortune on her education and in his eyes she should have aimed her sights higher by becoming a doctor or a lawyer. She was certainly bright enough, which meant she was also smart enough to know that happiness was more important than titles.

Hatter's was one of the most popular teashops in Threshold, and it was made to look topsy-turvy, there were chairs and tables all set up with tea things on the ceiling, whilst the tables on the floors were made to look like lampshades, and the chairs were giant moths. It gave Zoe a headache when she first started working there.

One of Zoe's work colleagues sidled up to her, and she did her best not to groan. Dawn was tall, pretty (even if she did wear too much make up, and hair been bleached too much).

"Zoe, do me a favour," Dawn whispered, "serve table thirteen for me."

Zoe sighed. The shop was busy because of half term, and between her and Mary, the other girl who served tables with them, they'd covered most of the tables. Although she enjoyed her job, she didn't like the idea of people taking advantage of her.

"If you want to go and see Mark then you can wait until Mary has been on her break," Zoe said firmly.

Mark was Dawn's boyfriend and worked in the garage not far from the shop. Zoe knew that, if Dawn went there now then she'd be missing for a couple of hours. Not that she'd get in to trouble because she was the owner's daughter. Zoe suppressed a sigh. It wasn't fair that she and Mary had to work twice as hard because Dawn wouldn't pull her weight.

"I don't want to see Mark," Dawn snapped. "It's that girl, the one with her back to us – I don't..." she tutted hard. "I just don't want to serve that table, okay?"

Zoe glanced over at the table and couldn't understand the problem. There was an old man, a chubby looking boy, a girl who looked a little bit like a scarecrow, and the girl Dawn was talking about; she had short, naturally blonde hair, and looked tiny compared to the other two Zoe guessed that she was their little sister. Zoe smiled sadly and wondered if they knew how lucky they were to have her. Nineteen years. Shouldn't it be easier after nineteen years? But every Christmas, every birthday there was a big gap in her life. A gap that grew and wouldn't ever be filled.

"Hello, Earth to Zoe!" Dawn smiled tightly. "Are you going to serve them for me?"

"What did she do?" Zoe asked. "Was she rude?"

"It's her face," Dawn whispered. "She's been in some sort of horrible accident... it makes me feel sick to look at it."

"Dawn! Bloody Hell! Sometimes you can be really horrible!" Zoe picked up her notepad and pen and hissed, "One day I hope karma will turn around and bite you on the ass."

As Zoe approached the table, she turned her frown into a polite smile and got her pen poised to take the group's order. She gave herself a mental pat on the back when she looked directly at the girl and managed to keep smiling. It wasn't that she found it horrible, it was more the thought of what the poor little thing had gone through to leave such terrible scars.

"Hello there," she said pleasantly, "my name is Zoe and I'm going to be serving you this afternoon. Would you like any drinks?" The man, scarecrow girl and the chubby boy looked nervous. The other little girl kept her eyes fixed firmly on the menu. Zoe blushed. 'Well this was awkward', she thought. "Would you like me to come back?"

The girl who was looking at the menu didn't look up,

her lips started moving, though no sound came out.

"Are you alright, sweetie?" Zoe asked.

"She's doing a spell," the boy said. "So no one around us can hear what we are talking about – it takes up a lot of concentration."

"Right." Zoe nodded slowly. Threshold was full of people who believed in magic. "Do you know what she would like to eat?"

"We're not here to eat, Zoe," said the scarecrow-girl. "We're here about your sister, India."

Zoe froze. It was like she'd been slapped. These children hadn't even been born when India had died.

"W... what about my sister?"

"My name is Megan," the girl said. "I can see ghosts and spirits and I live at Stone Towers. I haven't lived there very long. A few days ago I was in my garden and I heard someone crying in the hotel garden. It was India, she was..."

"Okay, stop right there!" Zoe turned to the man. "You sort of people make me sick! What makes you think I'd believe this rubbish?" Zoe was so angry that she could barely grab air. "And for your information, it's my Dad who has money and not me, so you can take you're little grief-profiteering group and get out. Just get the Hell out!"

"I don't want money," Megan said confused. "I want to help India cross over."

"Look, it's not going to work so you can stop this act right now," Zoe snapped.

"This isn't an act!"

"She thinks you're a cold reader," Roy said. "They're people who tell others that they can talk to the spirits of their loved ones – only at a price. They can't, all they do is read people's body-language and the subconscious reactions to what is being said to them."

"You were the one who told India about ghosts and spirits." Megan said.

"Lucky guess."

"You've got freckles on your shoulder that your Mum says looks like Orion," Megan offered.

"You could have seen that for yourself," Zoe snapped.

Megan desperately searched her memory for the special information India had give to her. She needed to get Zoe to believe her.

"On the nights your parents fought, India would climb into bed with you. You would sing to her, 'You're my sister, my lovely sister. I will love you every day, even when you're being a little monster. I'll never wish you away.' It would make her laugh.

A smile flitted across Zoe's mouth but was soon replaced by a hard cynical line.

"When the shouting was really bad you would sing her Brum's lullaby,"

A tear escaped Zoe's eye. "That's what India called Brahms lullaby," she croaked. Megan nodded her head, "And when she was sleepy, you would carry her back to her bed because ..."

Zoe raised a hand. "Please, please... stop. You said that India was crying. You said you wanted help to cross-over?"

"She didn't know she had... died." Megan said quietly. "She saw her Nan but she thought she'd fallen asleep and was dreaming. She stayed by the pond because your Mum told her that if she was ever lost she was to...."

"...wait for mummy. Mummy would come and find her," Zoe whispered. "God, it's been nineteen years! She's been waiting for Mum for nineteen years."

"India says you don't look too old."

Zoe emitted a noise that was half sob, half laugh. The man rummaged in his pocket and pulled out a packet of tissues, He handed her one.

"She doesn't want to see you cry," Megan told her.

"Where is she?"

Megan took Zoe's hand and pointed to her right.

"Can she hear me," Zoe asked.

Megan nodded.

"India?" Zoe felt awkward talking to thin-air in front of strangers. She blushed and Megan encouraged her on with a nod of the head. "I'm so sorry you've been waiting for so long. If I'd known that you were still in that garden, I would have come and got you – somehow."

"She knows that," Megan said. "She knows that you love her. India said that she'd really like to go and see Mummy, Daddy and Luke now."

"Okay." Zoe turned her attention to the girl casting the spell. She was looking very pale, and by her expression showed that she was suffering pain. "How long is she able to keep this up? She's not looking too good."

"Daisy!" Megan gasped. "Stop!"

Daisy dropped the menu. She was hyperventilating but at least the colour was returning to her cheeks.

"You said you weren't going to hurt yourself." Megan rushed to her side and threw her arm around her.

Scott grabbed hold of the girl's hand and looked concerned. It was obvious to Zoe that the boy had a sweetheart-crush on the girl.

"I didn't know Zoe was going to take so long to

convince," Daisy replied giving an apologetic smile.

"I'm sorry. This is all a bit out of the blue for me. My sister died a long time ago – I thought that part of my life was over. Look, I can get off my shift here; I'll say there's a family emergency – I guess it's kind of true. I'll meet you in the park in about half an hour." Zoe looked around to see if anyone had witnessed the strange events. Her eyes fell on the clock. The whole incident had taken just a minute or two

When Zoe returned to the counter Dawn was waiting for her with a curious look on her face. For a moment, Zoe worried that Dawn had somehow seen what had been happening. "They're leaving?"

Zoe turned around and feigned surprised. "I guess they changed their minds."

"Strange," Dawn said, chewing on the end of her pen. "Total bunch of weirdos if you ask me!"

"I don't think anybody did!" Zoe took her phone out of her pocket and pretended to be reading a received message. "Look, sorry," she said removing her pinny, "I've got to go: Family emergency!"

Before Dawn could ask anything further, Zoe had already left by the front door. She'd grab her bag and coat later – she had things she had to do first.

31 THE PARK

"I don't want you to ever do that to yourself again!" Megan said firmly.

They were sitting in Moon Crescent Park. It had a modest amount of woodland and lots of open green-space, picnic areas, three children's playgrounds, a miniature railway, meadows, and two big ponds. As soon as they entered the park, Daisy headed for the first tree they saw and sat down under it. She'd informed Megan that she was in desperate need of an 'energising cuddle.'

Daisy pulled her knees up to her chest, and rested her head on them, hiding her face. She looked so small and fragile. Scott sat down next to her and hesitated momentarily before putting his arm around her. Daisy responded to him, falling into the cup of his arm, leaving Megan to feel really quite awkward. She shook away the thought that maybe something was happening between Scott and Daisy.

Daisy lifted her head and offered Megan a tired smile.

It soon faded with the approach of Zoe.

"Hi," Zoe said. "Sorry I took longer than I thought, I'd forgotten how big this place was."

"Can we go and see Mummy, Daddy and Luke now?" India asked, holding Tabitha's hand.

"India wants to know if you're going to take us to see her family," Megan told her.

"We can go and see Mum first; she moved to Threshold to be closer to me," Zoe said.

"Where is India?" Zoe asked.

Megan put her hand just above India's head. Zoe turned but all she could see was thin air.

"God, I really wish I could see you. I've missed you so much, sweetheart. Before we go and see Mummy there's something you need to know." Zoe breathed in deeply, "Mummy and Daddy got divorced – like your friend Jimmy's Mummy and Daddy?"

Zoe remembered how upset India had been about that; probably because Jimmy was so upset rather than the fact that his parents had got divorced. Jim now ran his own photography business and was now engaged to Nancy, India's childhood best friend. If India had lived then it would probably have been her marrying Jim. Zoe quickly pushed the thought away; today wasn't about what might have been.

"Daddy ran away with the double glazing salesman!" India said, shocked.

It took Megan a moment to fully process what India was saying. She hesitated before translating, "She's asking if your Dad ran away with the double glazing salesman?"

Zoe giggled. "Well, okay, it's not *exactly* like Jimmy's Mummy and Daddy. Our mummy and daddy couldn't stop arguing."

India nodded. "I remember; and they used to throw things at each other and shout really loudly, but Zoe and Luke used to argue as well."

"I used to argue with my brother all the time," Tabitha said.

"What did Mummy and Daddy argue about?" India asked.

"Zoe, she wants to know what your parent's arguments were about." Megan said.

"Ah, okay, sweetie. Well, Mummy kept shouting at Daddy for drinking too much wine and Daddy kept shouting at Mummy for spending too much money on things that she didn't really need."

Tears ran down India's face. "I don't want them not to be together. Why didn't you and Luke fix them?"

"Because they couldn't." Tabitha knelt down and pulled India onto her lap. "If your Mummy and Daddy can't be friends anymore, there's nothing anyone can do to make it better."

"It's my fault," India said between hard sobs. "If I hadn't been naughty and gone near the water, I wouldn't have died and Mummy and Daddy wouldn't be sad, and they wouldn't be so angry at each other."

"She thinks that it's her fault that your parents have divorced." Megan told Zoe

"No!" Zoe's bottom lip quivered. "No, India! Never think that it's your fault. They are so sad that you died but Mummy and Daddy hadn't been friends for a very long time. They decided that it would be best not to stay together because it was making them really unhappy. They got tired pretending that everything was alright."

"So you live with Mummy, like Jimmy lived with his Mummy?" India asked.

"She wants to know if you live with your Mum?"

"No, Mummy lives near me though. Luke lives in London with his friends and Daddy still lives in Gloaming. We can go and see Mummy she doesn't live too far from here. We can walk."

Zoe looked at Daisy who'd gone back to resting her

head back on her knee. "Or we could get the bus?"

"No," Daisy said, raising her head, "I'll be alright." She stood up. "Let's get India to her Mummy."

32. MUMMY!

Hilary Banks (she absolutely refused to keep her married name) lived in flats that had been made to look like a Victorian mansion. Zoe had warned the group that her Mum would be very difficult to convince about India. Her Mum didn't believe in ghosts.

Hilary opened the door. She looked at Zoe and then at the group. Megan thought that Hillary Banks looked just like the bust of Nefertiti she'd once seen. She wore her long dark hair in a very tight bun.

"Hello." Her voice was high and crisp.

"Mum, this is Megan and her friends Daisy and Scott, and Scott's granddad, Roy."

"I'm here too Mummy," India shouted, jumping up and down.

"She can't see you sweetie," Tabitha reminded her gently. "Megan has to talk to her."

"Well," Hilary said, "you'd better come in I suppose."

They were led into the living room, which smelt strongly of furniture polish and musty potpourri. The walls were a warm green and the furniture was masculine, with black leather settees. Every available surface was covered with photographs.

"That's me," India said excitedly, pointing at a photograph of a baby.

"Could I get any of you a cup of tea or coffee?" Hilary asked " I've also got some squash. I think there might be some gingerbread left."

"Mum," Zoe said softly, "I think you should really sit down."

"Why? What's happened?"

"Ms Banks," Megan said, "my name is Megan and I live at Stone Towers." Hilary looked at her calmly and Megan swallowed hard. "I was in my garden when I heard crying coming from the hotel gardens. It was a little girl. Ms Banks, I can see ghosts and spirits and…"

"Exactly as I thought," Mrs Banks said sharply. She flashed her eyes towards Roy. "You should be ashamed of yourself getting children to do your dirty work."

"Mum, please listen to her."

Hilary stood up and took her daughter's hands in her own. "Sweetheart, I know you still miss your sister – I miss her too, but I thought we had got over this nonsense, especially after the Ouija incident in the school library."

"Mum, this is nothing like that!" Zoe protested. "Megan knows things I've never told anyone."

"Come on Zoe, you can't possibly remember every conversation you've ever had."

Hilary looked at Roy. "Take these children and get out of here."

"Mummy stole a pair of knickers," India shouted. "Tell her that she stole a pair of knickers."

"Do you remember telling anyone that you stole a pair of knickers?" Megan said quickly.

"I beg your pardon, what?"

"We were shopping for Nanny's funeral," India said. "Mummy wanted me to get a black dress. I didn't want a black dress I wanted a pink dress. Mummy said you don't wear pink to a funeral; she said it was rude.

"India said that she didn't like the black dress you brought. She wanted to wear the pink one but you told her that it was rude to wear pink at a funeral."

Hilary was staring at her. She wasn't moving – not even blinking.

Tabitha urged India to carry on. "Go on sweetie, finish the story."

India went red. "Mummy's knickers broke when we were looking for grey tights."

"She says that your knickers broke when you were looking for grey tights," Megan said. "You was wearing your nice suit because you were going to a meeting in the afternoon, they fell down and you said you couldn't walk round the shop without knickers on so you took a pair from the hanger, you said you would pay for them but forgot."

"You were dressed up nice and were wearing a skirt because you were going to a meeting in the afternoon." if Megan hadn't felt so desperate for Hilary to believe her she would have found it funny, "you felt uncomfortable so burrowed a pair from a hanger and forgot to pay for them."

"Mum, have you ever seriously told anyone that story?" Zoe asked.

Hilary said softly, "No, no I haven't."

"And you give me a lecture every time I eat a grape at a supermarket!"

"Megan?" India said quietly.

"Yes, sweetie?"

"Tell Mummy I'm sorry I told everybody her secret. Tell her I had to because she wasn't believing you."

"India would like you to know that she's sorry she told your…"

Megan was interrupted by Hilary's sobs. Zoe rushed over to her mother and wrapped her arms around her. Hilary crumpled into her daughter's shoulder.

"I'll make her a cup of tea," Roy said. "Where's the kitchen?"

Zoe pointed across the room and smiled a thank you.

"I'm so sorry I didn't believe you," Hilary choked. "I'm so sorry… She's here? Right now?"

"Mummy, don't cry!" India rushed over to her Mum and tried to put her hands onto her lap only to have them go straight through.

Hilary gasped. "My leg just went ice-cold!" She looked to Megan. "Did she just touch my leg?" Megan nodded. "Why is she still here and not in…?"

Megan bit her lip; Hilary was so upset that it was very difficult to tell her exactly why her little girl was still around. Perhaps the truth would hurt her even more than believing that ghosts never existed in the first place.

"She doesn't remember falling into the pond," Daisy said tenderly. "She thought she was lost and so she stayed where she was – that was what she had been told, and she was a good obedient little girl. She would still be waiting if it hadn't been for Megan."

"Mum, India has been waiting for us for nineteen

years!"

"Oh, my poor baby,"

At the sight of Hillary's tears, Megan thought on how her gift was more of a curse that caused pain than a gift that gave peace.

"My poor baby, India, I'm so sorry!"

"Please tell Mummy to stop crying," India said, wringing her hands together. "I'm okay! Tell her I'm okay!"

"She's asking you not to cry. She says that she's okay. Her Nan came to her but she didn't know whether to go or not. She wants you to give her permission to go."

Hillary nodded. "It's okay, India – go with Nanny – she'll look after you."

India shook her head sadly. "I don't want to leave you when you are sad."

"She doesn't want to leave you when you're sad."

Hilary smiled. "I'm happy to know that you're safe."

India turned to Tabitha. "I will see them again, won't I?"

"Of course you will," Tabitha said. "Remember, goodbyes aren't forever."

"I want to say goodbye to Daddy and Luke as well," India said.

"I think if India can say goodbye to her dad then she'll be able to cross-over." Megan told Hilary and Zoe.

Hillary shook her head, "I don't think Daddy will believe that you're still here."

"And Luke?" Megan asked.

"We haven't spoken to Luke since India died; we don't know where he is."

India frowned. "Zoe said he was living with friends in London."

Zoe shook her head. "That's not quite true. I know where he is. I couldn't blame him in the same way you did."

"That's not true, we never really blamed Luke." Hilary said with a frown.

Zoe shook her head again. "We all know that isn't true; you and Dad told him that if he hadn't been talking to those boys and had been watching India, as he'd been told, then she would never have drowned. He was only a child himself."

Roy came in from the kitchen and sensing the tension in the atmosphere stopped mid-pace. Tabitha was glaring at Hilary, and if the woman had been able to hear ghosts and spirits then she sure as Hell would have given Hilary a piece of her mind.

"But he tried to save her, didn't he?" Scott asked, remembering what he'd read in the newspaper. "How old was he?"

"Fifteen," Zoe said quietly.

"He dragged his little sister out of the pond and tried to save her and they blame him!" Tabitha said.

"We were both so upset, we didn't know what we were saying," Hilary protested, obviously not hearing what Tabitha said. She turned and looked at Roy – surely a father would understand. "I'd just lost my baby girl, I wasn't thinking properly I..."

"It wasn't Luke's fault!" India shouted and stamped her foot. The sound bounced off the floor making everyone jump.

"I thought ghosts couldn't touch anything?" Megan asked Tabitha.

"They can't, but when they're having strong feelings they can create enough energy to make a noise. Their emotions can affect the atmosphere around them."

"How?" Megan asked.

"I'm not sure," Tabitha replied. Megan gave her a look of disappointment and Tabitha became defensive. "We don't exactly get an instruction manual when we reach the afterlife, we learn what we can from each other."

The temperature in the flat went very cold. It was easy to see each other's breath.

"What's going on?" Hilary asked pulling Zoe protectively to her.

"I think it's fair to say that India is angry that you blame her brother for her death," Daisy replied.

"He was telling the boys to go away," India said. "I'd asked him to show me how to spin like a ballerina, he could dance just like a ballerina and he was brilliant, then the boys came and told him that only girls danced like that. They said he was girl. I told them to go away. I told them that he was the best boy in the whole world, and they laughed at me. Luke told me to go over to the pond and wait for me. He said he wouldn't be long. I went by the pond and was playing with my ball when I dropped it. I tried to get it but I fell in and I couldn't get out, I tried and tried and... Tabitha! Megan! I remember! I remember everything!"

"India now remembers what happened and she's really upset," Megan said. Megan relayed the events to Hillary and Zoe who sat in shock.

"Sounds like Luke thought that those boys were going to cause some trouble and didn't want his little sister caught up in it," Roy said passing Hilary a cup of tea. "Looks like what happened wasn't anyone's fault; not India's and not Luke's."

"It was an accident! Mummy and Daddy need to say sorry to Luke."

Megan looked at Zoe. "Do you think you could get Luke to come to Threshold?"

"I can talk to him," Zoe replied.

"If you knew where he was staying then why didn't you say anything?" Hilary asked.

"You've never actually asked! Neither has Dad." Zoe sighed. "Luke has been in some pretty big London shows and owns a really successful dance studio. He has a girlfriend who's really nice and they're planning on getting married next year."

Hillary brought her hand to her mouth and stifled the returning sobs.

"I guess you've missed out on a lot because you wouldn't listen," Zoe said, sadly.

"If you were so angry with me about it all then why did you stay in touch with me?" Hilary asked.

"Because you are my Mum," Zoe told her. "And I love you – enough to forgive you pretty much anything. That's what you do with the people you love, you accept them, for all of their faults."

Hilary's mouth opened to say something and then shut. Megan used the awkward break in conversation as an opportunity to get their attention back to helping India crossover.

"Could you get your Dad to come to Threshold?" she asked Zoe.

"I'll tell him that I've got some exciting news. I won't be able to tell him that Mum and Luke are going to be there: he wouldn't come."

"Okay, I think it'll be nice for India to say goodbye to her family in the last place where she last saw them," Megan said. "My parents don't know I have this ability so it's a bit difficult."

"I'll give you my number," Roy said to Hilary. "Scott can then phone Megan when we've got a plan together."

"Maybe Hilary should be around when Zoe calls Luke," Daisy suggested.

Hilary squeezed Zoe's hand and gave her a small smile. All Megan could hope for now was that Zoe would be able to convince her brother and Dad to come, and then hopefully India would be able to crossover. Megan couldn't help but cross her fingers.

33. GRANDDAD

Daisy sat down next to her Granddad's bedside and gently took his hand between her own. She loved his hands; they were big and the fingers looked clumsy but she remembered how he used to take her hand as though it was made of china, and sometimes those fingers would delicately pull a thorn from her fingers when they used to pick blackberries. It was skin that used to be tanned by the weather but was now as white as snow and just as cold. Underneath his fingernails the skin was a faint blue colour. If Patrick Monroe knew someone was holding his hand he didn't show it. His eyes remained closed and his breaths out were much longer than his breaths in.

"Hi," Daisy said quietly. "I know you don't remember me but I'm your granddaughter Daisy."

The room was quiet except for the soft gurgling sound that came from the back of Patrick's throat. Daisy brought his hand to her lips and gently blew on the fingers, rubbing them just as he had done to her when she was cold as a baby

"You've forgotten all about me but I haven't forgotten you, so I've come to sit with you for a little while, okay?" she said, although she knew she wasn't going to get an answer. "My friend Megan has The Glow... you've probably forgotten what that is; it's when someone can see ghosts and spirits, well I'm helping her to understand it so she's not so afraid. I think I'm doing an okay job. There's a boy called Scott who's a Bland but he's our friend and he is also helping her - you know, making sure she doesn't feel like a complete freak." Daisy placed Patrick's hand onto the side of her face, the side that wasn't scarred. "She's helping the ghost of a little girl to cross-over; she drowned you see but didn't remember and thought she was lost. She was always told that if you were lost you should stay right where you were and then someone could come and find you. She'd been waiting nineteen years! We think the reason she hasn't crossed-over yet is because she needs to say goodbye to her family. We've managed to get her Mum and sister to believe and they told us the brother is pretty opened minded so that shouldn't be a problem, but it's the Dad... he sounds like a jerk! I can sense the hurt and pain coming from the Mum and sister and I don't think it's only because of the little girl drowning. The parents blamed the brother for it, you see. He was only fifteen. But he was the one who tried to save his little sister, he tried to bring her back but they still blamed him because he was distracted by some bullies: It's sad."

She placed his hand back onto the bed and turned it over so the palm was facing upwards. It felt warmer. She traced the lines with her finger and then drew circles in the centre, reminding her of when he had used to sing; 'Walk around the garden, like a teddy bear, a one step, a two-step and…' A sob escaped Daisy's lips, catching her by surprise. Tears pricked her eyes and she wiped them away angrily, clearing her throat trying to get rid of the lump.

"Sorry, I'm just being a baby. Crying never helped anyone, did it?" She coughed again annoyed at how weepy her voice sounded. "I think we're going to be able to help the little girl to cross over and I was thinking that I wouldn't have been able to help Megan as much as I have if you hadn't taught me so much; I just wanted to say thank you. I miss you, Granddad, and I love you so much. I don't know if you can hear me and I know you don't know who I am but I just want to say it's okay to go – that's if you want to. I'll be sad because you won't be here anymore but I'd like to think that wherever you go, you'll be watching me and remember who I am... Granddad? Please remember who I am."

There was a gentle tap on the door that made Daisy turn. It was Una. She looked tired which made her look much older. She smiled at Daisy but Daisy could see that her eyes were red from where she had been crying. She had been doing that a lot recently, especially when she thought Daisy couldn't hear her. Daisy guessed it was because it didn't matter that granddad had been ill for a very long time and that he'd forgotten who his wife was, she still loved him. Daisy hoped Una hadn't heard everything she'd said. She hadn't really wanted Daisy to sit on her own with Patrick, but Daisy had said that she had to say something to him, something private.

"Daisy, sweetheart, Scott is on the phone. Would you like me to tell him to call back?"

Daisy shook her head. "No, I've finished here," she said quietly. She placed Patrick's hand under the bedcovers, stood up and kissed her granddad on the forehead. "Night, granddad, I love you."

She waited for a second, just hoping that she would see him smile or open his eyes, when nothing happened, she took a deep breath and left the room.

34. GOODBYE

"Do you think Daisy is okay?" Scott whispered.

They were standing where Megan had seen India for the very first time. Next to them were Zoe, Hilary and Luke. Luke looked different from the photographs they'd seen in Hilary's flat, of course he looked a lot older, still handsome, but he had shaved off his hair, making him look harder. When his Mum stared at his bald head he'd explained that his hair had been thinning and he thought it looked much better having no hair at all than trying to cling to the few strands left. He had politely shook everyone's hand and then asked Megan where his baby sister was.

India was standing on the other side of Megan, holding onto Tabitha's hand. When Megan pointed, he crouched down, remembering her eye level.

"Hey, princess," he had said ever so softly. "Sorry you had to wait so long for someone to come and get you."

"It wasn't your fault, Luke," India replied. "It was an accident. I'm sorry Mummy and Daddy was angry with you so such a long time. I love you."

Megan repeated what India said and Luke looked like he was going to burst into tears. He blew a kiss in India's direction and told her that he loved her too.

As Luke, Zoe and Hilary talked to one another, Megan moved closer to Scott and looked at Daisy who had gone and sat at the other side of the garden reading the book Scott had given her. She wanted to be around in case they needed a spell but she didn't think that a big group meeting would be a good idea; goodbyes should be as private as possible.

"Is she alright?" Megan whispered.

Scott shook his head. "I don't think her Granddad is doing too good."

The rain clouds looked heavy but there was still no sign of them emptying any time soon. When the wind blew, it felt as though there were little knives in it, cutting any skin that was bare.

"Do you think my Daddy is coming?" India asked hopefully.

Tabitha shrugged.

Zoe had told them that she'd spoken to their father, Richard but she wasn't sure how he was going to take it. She'd asked to him to come and talk to her face to face and insisted that he come and meet her in the hotel garden. He had been reluctant and pushy to know the reasons why but she refused to tell him. Megan didn't feel very positive about the whole situation.

"Maybe he's in the bar." Hilary sighed and looked at Zoe. "Do you think you should go and check?"

Zoe was just about to walk towards the hotel when she stopped. A solid looking man with a neatly trimmed beard, and a thatch of thick grey hair was heading towards them. He looked tired; his face was puffy and he had red cheeks and nose. He took his time to glare at each of them and then shook his head in disgust. He didn't say a word, just turned and started to walk away.

"Dad, please wait!" Zoe shouted. "This is about India! This is what India would want."

Richard Cole stopped and seemed to count to ten before turning around and walking stiffly back towards them.

"Hello, Hilary," he said coolly.

"Richard." Hilary replied folding her arms protectively across her chest. "Luke's here…"

Richard didn't acknowledge his son, it was as if he were invisible.

"It wasn't his fault that India drowned, Mr Cole,"

Megan said. "Those boys he was talking too were bullying him because he was showing India how he could dance. Luke didn't want India to get upset. He told her to wait for him. She went by the pond and dropped the ball in and when she tried to reach for it... It was an accident."

Mr Cole didn't soften. He threw a glance at Luke and spat out, "If he hadn't been prancing about then those boys wouldn't have had any reason to be bullying him. And by the way, just who the Hell are you?"

"Don't talk to the child like that," Zoe said firmly. "This is Megan. She can see ghosts. She lives..."

"Right!" Richard replied giving Zoe a look of utter disappointment. He then looked at Hilary accusingly, clearly of the mind that all of this was his ex-wife's ludicrous idea. "And you actually believed this?"

"Not at first," Hilary replied, "but she was able to tell me things only India would know. And Luke and I are talking so that must tell you something."

"It tells me that these she's a very accomplished actress. I didn't know con-artists started so young!" Richard looked at Scott, "And who are you supposed to be, her agent? Bodyguard?"

"I'm..." Scott started.

"It doesn't matter." Richard shook his head and looked

back at his ex-wife. "Hilary when someone is desperate, they believe anything. You of all people know that. How much have they asked for?"

"You know there used to be a time when you would have believed what I said," Hilary said.

Mr Cole let out a cruel snort of a laugh. "Yes, well that was before the bailiffs started knocking at the door after you promised me you wouldn't spend anymore."

"I should have told Mummy that he hit Luke," India said angrily.

"You hit Luke!" Megan said.

"What?" Hilary gasped, fixing Mr Cole with an accusing eye. "When?"

"When he saw Luke copying the people dancing on the television and you and Zoe were at the doctors," India said. "Daddy had been drinking wine and he said that real men didn't dance. He said they were girls in boy's bodies. Luke said that was rubbish. Daddy told him he was talking back, and he hit him: he hit him really hard. Luke went into the wall and hit his face. Daddy told him to say that he'd done it in P.E."

Megan repeated what India had said trying not to miss anything out. India let go of Tabitha's hand and walked over to Richard.

"I was there when you hit Luke, Daddy. I cried and I cried because you hurt him and I ran up to my bedroom. You came in and said if I told what happened, you would take my rabbit to the vets and have her put down."

"India says she saw you hit Luke," Megan said. "You told her that if she told anyone what she saw, you would have her rabbit put down."

Richard went pale. There was no way this girl could know this. He'd made sure that he had kept his voice down, leaving Luke alone to deal with his bloody nose at the kitchen sink. Even after all these years he still remembered that day. He hadn't been that drunk not to know what had happened, and he had waited months for Hilary to find out the truth of Luke's bruised cheek. He'd waited for the screaming and shouting... and then India had drowned.

"India?" he whispered. "I'm so sorry."

India turned to Megan and looked at her sadly. "Daddy always said if you said sorry for something that you kept doing, then you weren't really sorry. And he kept being a bully. He wasn't sorry." Something caught her attention and she turned around and gasped. "Oh wow, what's that?"

"That is the light and it's going to take you to a very special place," Tabitha said. "It means that it's alright for you to come with me."

"It's pretty," India whispered. She looked back at her family. "Are they going to be alright?"

"India is ready to cross-over now," Megan said. "But she's worried about leaving you behind."

"We'll be fine, Sweetheart," Hilary said, taking hold of Zoe and Luke's hand. "Just fine."

"Thank you, Megan," India said.

Tabitha took India's hand and lead her to the light. India looked back at her family one last time.

"It's okay, Sweetie, goodbyes aren't for ever, remember?" She pointed. "See?"

India burst out laughing, "Nanny! I'm coming Nanny!"

And she ran with her arms outstretched ready to hug someone.

Then she was gone.

35. IT'S OKAY.

Having said goodbye to India's family, the small group went over to Daisy who was waiting for them. Megan put her hands in her pocket. Even though she was wearing gloves the tips of her fingers were still cold.

"I didn't think that helping a ghost cross-over would involve being so...." Scott tried to find the right word.

"Angry?" Megan suggested. "She was so angry with her dad but I can understand why. He's really horrible isn't he? I thought it would be more about forgiving people rather than just letting them kind of know you were pissed at them."

"It's not always like that," Tabitha replied, lighting a cigarette. "Maybe it'll make him try and make it up to Zoe and Luke, though I can't blame them if they don't want anything to do with him,"

"Is India gone?" Daisy asked.

"Yeah," Megan nodded, "her Nan was there to meet

her."

Daisy smiled. "That's great." She held up the book. "Scott, I'm not going to lie, this is great, there's only a few mistakes but I can help you there."

Something appeared next to Megan, making her jump. It took her a moment to place the figure that had emerged.

"Seriously?" Tabitha asked the figure. "She's only just helped a little kid cross-over, couldn't you even wait a day?"

"It's alright, Tabitha," Megan said quietly.

She knew this man; she'd met him only once, lying in a bed confused and blind, thinking his granddaughter was his daughter. He looked kind of the same, only there was no sign of him ever having had a stroke. He looked fit and healthy and was looking directly at Megan.

"Sorry," he said. "This honestly won't take long, Megan."

Megan nodded.

"Megan, who is it?" Scott asked

"Daisy," she said quietly, "Oh, Daisy I'm so sorry."

"Granddad?" Daisy asked. Megan nodded. "It's okay Megan, I knew he didn't... that he wasn't..." She shook her head and cleared her throat, that horrible lump was back. "Hello Granddad."

"Hello, sweetheart," Patrick said. "I really wish you could hear me."

"He wishes that you could hear him," Megan said. "Listen, I'll repeat everything he says."

Patrick smiled gratefully and moved closer to his granddaughter.

"I may have forgotten you in my mind, Daisy but I never forgot you in my heart. I'm going to miss my little nurse. You're such a good girl, Daisy; you're kind and clever, and you're growing up to be a remarkable woman – just remember, you don't have to grow up too quickly. You can't save the whole world, but you can do little things to make it better, which is just as good. You don't always have to be everyone's rock; it's okay to be sad, and it's okay to cry – crying helps you know, it stops things hurting quite so much and it shows the world that you need to be taken care of now and again."

Albie appeared next to Patrick and looked up at him, tail wagging. Small, hard drops of rain starting falling from the sky.

"Goodbye, Daisy," Patrick said before turning around and disappearing.

"He's gone, isn't he?" Daisy asked.

Megan nodded.

Daisy's eyes filled with tears. "I don't know what I'm going to do without him," she whispered.

Together, Megan and Scott wrapped her up into a comforting hug, making her feel safe and loved, and for the first time in years Daisy Monroe let herself cry.

THE END.

ABOUT HELEN WHAPSHOTT

Helen was born in Aldershot in the year of 1980. She survived the infant, junior and senior schools of Cove. Helen started her working life in a bakery before deciding catering wasn't really for her that she wanted to work in the care industry.

After attending Farnborough College of Technology, where she did her diploma in nursery nursing she took on a variety of roles that included being a Nursery Nurse, a Special Needs Teaching assistant, a support worker for people with special need and a care assistant in a nursing home.

She's worked as a Health Care Assistant at a local hospital for eight years and also works as a bank carer at a children's hospice in surrey.

Helen has always loved stories, ever since her Mum used to read Hans Christian Anderson and Roald Dahl to her at bedtime. When she learnt to read by herself she couldn't get enough of books becoming a big fan of authors such as Arthur Conan Doyle's, Sherlock Holmes stories, as well as Neil Gaiman and Ben Aaronovitch.

With a love of reading came a love of creative writing. She recalls how her first hit was, "How The Kangaroo Got It's Hop, at infant school when I was six, but I missed out on seeing my classmate's enjoyment because I was off several weeks with the mumps; when I got back the hype had died down. A disappointment I've never really gotten over! Being able to share my creations this time and is a dream come true."

www.helenwhapshott.weebly.com

Made in the USA
Charleston, SC
28 November 2016